THE GREAT ELEPHANT CHASE

THE
GREAT
ELEPHANT
CHASE

Gillian Cross

Oxford University Press
Oxford Melbourne Toronto

Oxford University Press, Walton Street,
Oxford OX2 6DP

*Oxford New York Toronto
Delhi Bombay Calcutta Madras Karachi
Petaling Jaya Singapore Hong Kong Tokyo
Nairobi Dar es Salaam Cape Town
Melbourne Auckland*

and associated companies in
Berlin Ibadan

Oxford is a trade mark of Oxford University Press

Copyright © Gillian Cross 1992
First published 1992

ISBN 0 19 271672 7

A CIP catalogue record for this book is available
from the British Library

Typeset by Pentacor PLC, High Wycombe,
Bucks
Printed in Great Britain

Author's Note

While I was writing this book, I received invaluable help from many people and organizations. I am extremely grateful to all of them and, in particular, to:

The American Swedish Institute, Minneapolis, Minnesota
Monica and Martin Arnold
Campus Martius/Ohio River Museum, Marietta, Ohio
Cass County Historical Society, Plattsmouth, Nebraska
The Cincinnati Historical Society, Cincinnati, Ohio
Harold Warp Pioneer Village, Minden, Nebraska
The Historical Society of Pennsylvania, Philadelphia, Pennsylvania
Professor M.L. Huffines
Illinois Historical Survey, Urbana, Illinois
Information Services/IRAD, Illinois State Archives, Springfield, Illinois
The Institute of Historical Research, University of London
Nebraska State Historical Society, Lincoln, Nebraska
Stuhr Museum of the Prairie Pioneer, Grand Island, Nebraska
Dr A.E.P. Twort

They helped me to imagine what the United States was like at the end of the nineteenth century, and I thank them all very much.

But they are not responsible for the Tamaquon River and Markle, Pennsylvania; nor for Eastcote's Landing and Albery, Nebraska. Do not look for those places on any map except the one in this book.

Gillian Cross

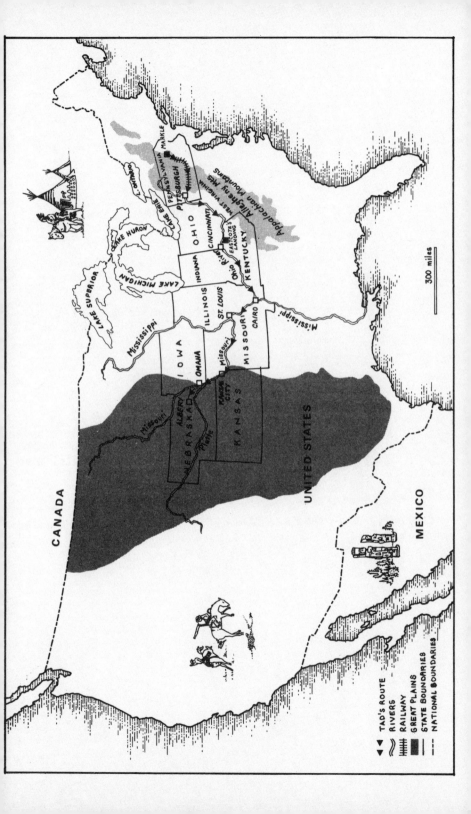

CHAPTER 1

IT WAS the first of April when Tad looked out of the upstairs window.

He didn't often look. Markle was a dirty, dreary town, and he'd had fifteen years to study the view. Grimy river flats. Long lines of miners' houses crawling up Horsehead Mountain. And the Number One coal-breaker of the Tamaquon Valley and East Pennsylvania Coal Company—a hundred-foot wooden tower that crunched up coal and spewed gritty dust over the valley.

But, that morning, something caught his eye as he passed the window with Mr Levington's dirty breakfast tray. He stopped at the top of the stairs and turned back.

The mountain was crowded with miners and their wives and children, all scurrying downhill as fast as they could go, in a scatter of coloured neckerchiefs and gaudy shawls and garish bonnets. Where were they going? Tad was too far away to hear anything, but he saw them waving and laughing to each other.

He was still staring when Esther, the hired girl, came creeping out of the second back-bedroom. The one that Mr Jackson rented. When she saw Tad she jumped, and her eyes narrowed.

'What are you doing there?'

'Just looking.'

'You've got no business to be looking!'

'But there's something strange—'

'Strange?'

Esther pushed him out of the way, impatiently, and looked out of the window. When she saw the crowd, she took a step nearer, her face sharp with curiosity.

'What's happening?' Tad said, forgetting to be careful of her. 'Is it an important day?'

1

'None of your business,' snapped Esther, staring out of the window. 'Get down and help your aunt with the breakfast!'

'But that's your job.'

He should have known better. Esther's mouth twisted irritably. Whirling round, she gave him a sudden, spiteful push. Tad was taller than she was, but he was off guard, and holding a tray. He jerked, caught his foot in the edge of the carpet and went tumbling down the stairs in a shower of cutlery and crumbs and pieces of rose-patterned china.

Aunt Adah was just coming out of the kitchen with the boarders' breakfast. He hit her, square on, and ham and eggs and hot cakes flew up into the air and splattered down on to the Brussels carpet. More rose-patterned china fell too, crunching into hundreds of fragments.

'Thaddeus Hawkins!' Aunt Adah stepped back, out of the mess, and turned purple.

Tad scrambled to his feet. 'I didn't—'

But he was interrupted by a scornful voice. 'You know what he's like, Miss Hawkins.' Esther came down the stairs, picking her way over the broken china. 'Wasn't looking where he was going. Came to the top of the stairs and tumbled straight down.'

She was so cool that it took Tad's breath away. He opened his mouth to argue, but before he could say a word he saw a dark shape following her. Mr Jackson had come out of his room. He started to walk down towards them, with slow, heavy steps.

'Lucky not to break his neck,' he said, in the thick voice that made Tad shiver. 'Boy's not quite right in the head, if you ask me.'

His bloodshot eyes gazed down at Tad, daring him to argue, and Aunt Adah threw her hands in the air.

'Fifteen years old, and not an ounce more sense than the day he was born. As if he didn't do enough damage *that* day.'

The other four boarders had crowded into the dining-room doorway. She put on her tragic, mournful face and they tutted sympathetically and glared at Tad.

2

He looked down. 'Sorry, ma'am. About the carpet. And the breakfast. And the china. And—'

He could never do enough apologizing. All day long there were things he broke and muddled and spoilt, and even when he'd said sorry for all of those he wasn't square. He'd been wrong from the day he was born.

Aunt Adah folded her arms. 'Words won't mend it. You'll have to get down on your hands and knees and do out the hallway, from top to bottom.'

'Yes, ma'am,' Tad said. He had expected that.

Esther was ready for it, too. As soon as Aunt Adah finished speaking, she broke in eagerly.

'We're fresh out of ammonia, ma'am. I'll go down to the store and get some more.'

'Oh no you won't!' Aunt Adah snapped. 'I'll need you to cook the breakfast all over again. Tad will have to go to the store himself.'

'But he'll only—'

'I said Tad will go!'

There was a second of frozen silence.

Esther tossed her head and turned an ugly red, but Aunt Adah ignored her.

'You must ask for three quarts of ammonia,' she said to Tad. 'Tell him I'll pay at the end of the week, and be careful when you're carrying it back.'

Tad nodded and she bustled away, leaving the boarders to drift back to the breakfast table. Esther crossed the hall, kicking Tad's ankle as she passed.

'That's for sneaking round your aunt! You were just itching to get out and see what was going on, weren't you?'

'Of course not. Aunt Adah just—'

'Well, she won't be able to order *me* around much longer!' Esther smirked, and disappeared into the kitchen.

Mr Jackson had just reached the bottom of the stairs. He watched Esther go, with a strange, small smile, and then he turned to go into the dining-room.

As he went by, he put a big, clammy hand on Tad's arm. 'You'll never come to anything,' he said, in his thick voice.

3

The idea seemed to amuse him. 'You don't know how to look out for yourself. If you don't take what you want, no one's going to give it to you. Try taking lessons from Esther.'

Tad shuddered. He couldn't help himself. The pads of Mr Jackson's fingers were pressing into his elbow, like the feet of some gross reptile.

With a smile of satisfaction, Mr Jackson let go and pushed past, into the dining-room. Thankfully, Tad opened the front door and breathed in the fresh, clean air.

He had almost forgotten about the crowd on the mountain, but he remembered as soon as he stepped outside. There was a loud babble of voices coming from round the corner, in Main Street. He slipped up the alley, expecting to see a crowd.

But it was no ordinary crowd. The size of it took his breath away.

There were hundreds of people, pushing and scurrying and hurrying past. Old Mrs Bobb. The Pritchard children. Mrs Keyser. All the Rinehimers were together, chattering as they went, and Mr Garringer was coming out of the offices of the *Tamaquon Valley Mercury* with his notebook in his hand.

It seemed as though everyone was there, heading for the railroad depot. And they were all talking about the same thing. One word—whispered or giggled or shouted—came at Tad from every side.

Elephant.

The whole town was turning out, and there was only one thing in people's minds.

. . . *going to see the elephant* . . . *heard it's a huge elephant* . . . *can there really be an elephant?* . . .

Tad grabbed at Dolly Preston's arm.

'What's happening? Where are you going?'

Dolly looked down her nose, but she condescended to answer. 'There's a man come to the depot with an elephant. They say he's giving rides.'

'A *real* elephant?'

But Dolly had twitched her arm free and gone on. Tad looked down Main Street, towards the store where Aunt Adah had sent him. Then he looked up, towards the depot.

4

Elephant.

He had never seen an elephant. And what was it Mr Jackson had said? *A person has to look out for himself.*

He looked up the road again. The crowd was solid, all the way from the bank to the depot, and he hadn't got time to tag on behind. But maybe he could get round the back way.

He ducked down the alley opposite, between the Sively house and Mason's store, and began to run along the rear of the lots, towards the railroad. But even then he couldn't get close to the tracks. The crowd had flooded out of the depot and there was a line of people, eight to ten deep, all the way along.

It was impossible to see over their heads, so Tad began to work his way through, looking for spaces and wriggling into them. When a gap opened, all the way to the front, he put his shoulder into it and pushed.

His feet tangled with a walking stick. Staggering, he pitched forward, and bumped into someone in the front row. Before he could get his balance, old Mrs Bobb reached over from behind and rapped him on the head.

'Thaddeus Hawkins! You ought to be ashamed!'

'I—I—' Tad cowered away from her hand. 'Sorry, ma'am.'

'Is no use to apologize to *me!*' Mrs Bobb hit him again. 'You want that people think we are savages in Markle? Barbarians, who knock over cripples? Hey?'

Tad blinked, looked round—and saw the girl he had bumped into.

She was thirteen or fourteen, but very small, with a narrow face and pale, gleaming ringlets. Everything about her was neat and well-made, from her blue cloth dress to her shining buttoned boots.

Except for the ugly wooden crutches that held her up.

She had been knocked off balance, and the young woman next to her, who seemed barely old enough to be her mother, was hauling her back on to her feet.

Mrs Bobb tutted loudly and people began to stare at Tad.

'It is that nephew of Adah Hawkins's,' Mrs Rinehimer said. 'He pushes a cripple out of the way.'

5

Mr Garringer shook his head. 'That boy! Always in some kind of trouble!'

Tad could hardly speak for embarrassment. 'I'm sorry,' he muttered gruffly. 'Did I hurt you?'

The mother frowned, but the girl looked up at Tad with a sweet, angelic smile. Almost too perfect to be true.

'Don't fret. It didn't hurt at all. I can't feel much.'

Mrs Rinehimer sighed sympathetically and Tad shuffled his feet, feeling large and clumsy and uncouth. The girl was smiling at him kindly enough, but she was the only one.

Then, suddenly, everything changed, with a great gasp of breath that started at the depot and came sighing down the tracks. The whole crowd turned to look right, and people began pushing and craning their necks. Tad turned too, but for a moment all he could make out was a forest of heads.

And then he saw the elephant.

It came ambling along the front of the crowd, between the main track and the siding. Its huge feet moved delicately over the rough stones and, from high on its neck, a miner waved a nervous hand.

'Only twenty cents for an unforgettable experience!' said a voice like a trumpet. 'Take a ride on the elephant and feel, for yourself, man's domination of the greatest creature on earth!'

The elephant had almost reached Tad before he saw who was shouting. It was a short, flamboyant figure in a tall hat and a jacket lined with scarlet silk. He strode ahead, waving one arm dramatically and leading the elephant on a short length of frayed rope.

The elephant.

It passed close to Tad, not five paces away. Its side was like a wall of rock, grooved with a thousand interwoven wrinkles. A few hairs sprouted from the rock, like lichens on an ancient crag, and the ripe, grassy smell of elephant flesh filled the air.

Tad was mesmerized. If Mrs Bobb had hit him with a mallet, he wouldn't have noticed. If the girl with the crutches had burst into song, he wouldn't have heard. He couldn't take his eyes from the great, slow body of the elephant.

The elephant stopped, twenty yards further up the line, to

let the miner dismount. As it turned back towards Tad, he looked up into its face, at the small, remote eye, almost hidden in a cocoon of wrinkles.

' . . . most wondrously loyal and intelligent creatures!' the man in the tall hat bellowed, almost in Tad's ear. 'Capable of understanding a vast range of commands . . . '

Tad's eyes travelled over the humped head and down the long line of the trunk, to the massive legs. The nearest foot was thicker than his whole body, with gnarled yellow toenails the size of his fist.

The great foot took one more step, and the man in the tall hat raised his voice, suddenly and sharply.

'But still I have not revealed the most amazing fact about Khush—'

He paused, as though to gather everyone's attention. It was a dramatic silence, and even Tad took his eyes off the elephant and looked round, for a second.

And in that second, the elephant moved. The long, grey trunk snaked down—so close to Tad that it brushed his cheek—and looped itself round the girl with the crutches. Before anyone could react, it lifted her high into the air.

CHAPTER 2

THERE WAS a gasp, a buzz of whispers—and then a fearful, petrified silence. Everyone in the crowd gazed up at the unconscious girl in the elephant's trunk. Her hair had fallen over her face, and her skirt was hitched up, showing the loops of scarlet ribbon in her frilly white drawers.

I should have done something, Tad thought. He stared up at the elephant, but its face was blank. Incomprehensible. Everyone was waiting for the showman to speak, but he was staring as hard as anyone else.

It was the girl's mother who broke the silence.

'Get her down.' The whisper was more terrifying than a scream. 'She has a weak heart. *Get her down.*'

Mrs Bobb gasped and there was a murmur of sympathy. The showman stepped forward.

'Keep calm, dear lady. Your daughter is not in danger.' He put a hand on the young woman's shoulder. 'I can get her down, but I must have silence.' He raised his voice, speaking to the whole crowd. '*Complete* silence, if you please.'

It came, uncannily fast. For a hundred yards, on each side, the tracks were lined with silent people. There was nothing to be heard except the grinding of the coal-breakers, away on Horsehead Mountain.

The showman took a step back and waved his stick at the elephant, its little steel tip glinting in the morning sunlight.

'Khush! Down!'

The elephant's eyes flickered, but it did not move.

The man rapped the stick on the ground and spoke more sharply. 'Khush! No!'

For an instant, no one breathed and Tad's chest was tight with fear. Then, very slowly, the thick trunk began to uncurl. The elephant lowered the girl towards the ground and the showman took her into his arms, with her head flopping back and her eyes closed.

'Is she—dead?' The young woman stretched out a shaking arm.

'Not dead, ma'am.' The showman's voice carried over the crowd. 'The shock to her nervous system has put her into a catalepsy. But I can cure that, if you will allow me.'

'You will let him touch her?' Mrs Bobb muttered.

'Anything!' The mother clutched at the showman's arm. '*Anything* that will bring her to herself!'

He smiled down at her. 'Could I trouble you to fetch my bag from the depot?'

As if in a daze, the young woman walked off down the tracks, and Mrs Bobb looked disapprovingly at the elephant.

'Is not good they leave her near that Creature.'

There was a rumble of agreement, but it died away quickly as the mother came back with a battered leather bag. She held it out to the showman and he nodded.

'There is a bottle at the bottom. Can you find it?'

The woman pulled out a small, corked bottle made of clear glass, lifting it high in the air, so that everyone saw. Kneeling down, the showman laid the unconscious girl across his lap and took a little silver spoon from his pocket.

'If you would fill the spoon? Thank you, ma'am. And now, perhaps, if you would open her mouth? Thank *you*.'

Slowly, giving everyone round him the chance to observe, he tipped the green liquid into the girl's mouth.

'Don't know about bringing her round,' muttered Mr Garringer. 'He'll be lucky if she doesn't choke.'

But she didn't choke. She swallowed twice, with her eyes still closed, and stirred slightly. Her mother took a step forward.

'No!' the showman said sharply. 'This tincture is perfectly safe, but it is strong. *You must not touch her.*'

As he spoke, the limp girl in his arms went suddenly stiff. The body arched backwards, rigid from top to toe, her outstretched arms clenched into fists and her lips drew back from her teeth, as if she were in torment.

'It is a fit!' wailed Mrs Rinehimer.

'Keep back!' shouted the man. 'No one must touch her!'

The spasm lasted for almost a minute. Then the girl slumped and her eyelids fluttered open.

'Mama? What—?'

'It's all right, Cissie,' the young woman said. 'You're safe now. The kind gentleman rescued you from the elephant.'

'Kind?' spluttered Mr Rinehimer. 'When it is his elephant that has caused the trouble?'

'The animal ought to be shot,' said Mrs Pritchard. 'It's too big to be safe.'

There was a murmur of agreement from the crowd and the showman stood up, with Cissie still in his arms.

'I do assure you that this elephant is *not* dangerous. He knows he has done wrong. See how he hangs his head!'

It was true. As he spoke, the elephant's head dropped and it shuffled its feet. The man looked down at Cissie.

'If—out of the kindness of your heart—you could go to Khush and give him a pat, he will know he is forgiven. I promise he will not hurt you.'

Cissie's mouth trembled, but she nodded, her pale face very solemn. The showman set her on her feet and she walked to the elephant's side. Slowly she raised her hand and patted one enormous front leg.

'Dear little soul,' muttered Mrs Pritchard.

Mrs Keyser nodded. 'She is brave as a lion.'

Everyone whispered approvingly—until Mrs Bobb shrieked. Suddenly, in the middle of the murmurs, her voice rang out. 'She walks! She is on crutches before, but now—she walks!'

Bending down, she picked up one of the wooden crutches lying beside Tad and waved it at the crowd. Cissie looked at her feet and then looked up, with a smile of amazement, and the young woman shrieked even louder than Mrs Bobb.

'She hasn't walked for five years! Not since she had the fever!'

The crowd went wild. People elbowed forward to examine the crutches, and to watch Cissie walk, and to look at the magic green tincture in the little bottle. Tad was pushed right across the tracks, towards the miners' houses, by people who shouted as they shoved.

'Cousin Amy's boy could try it!'

'Sally Helmslow, that fell off the barn when she was twelve . . . '

' . . . my father . . . '

Above the voices, the man in the tall hat bellowed his explanations.

' . . . an ancient remedy from India. I make it in large quantities for the elephant. It contains stored electrical impulses . . . works directly on the nervous system . . . '

Tad stood on tiptoe, trying to catch a glimpse of what was happening—and he saw Esther.

She was in the crowd, not ten yards away from him, hanging on Mr Jackson's arm. He was bending over to whisper in her ear, with his fleshy lips close to her hair, and she looked scarlet and triumphant.

Tad didn't know what they were doing there, together, but he knew it would mean trouble if they saw him. They both knew he was meant to be at the store. And both of them would enjoy telling Aunt Adah he had sneaked off to see the elephant instead . . .

He sidled away from them, towards a big railroad car that stood on the siding. It was painted bright red, with high, slatted sides, and florid gold letters ran from one end to the other.

MICHAEL KEENAN'S GREAT ELEPHANT SHOW!!

He meant to duck down behind it, and he edged round the lowered ramp, peering at the turnips and bales of hay heaped up inside.

But then, out of the corner of his eye, he saw Esther turn in his direction. Without thinking, he bolted up the ramp, into the wagon. His feet thudded on the wooden floor, and his heart thudded harder. Desperate for cover, he squeezed in among the hay bales at the far end, pulling them round to hide him.

At every moment, he expected to see Esther in the

doorway, pointing her finger spitefully at him. And Mr Jackson, standing behind her, with a fat grin on his face. But they didn't come.

It was the crowd that trapped him.

Suddenly, everyone surged back from the depot towards the wagon. Tad's hiding place, which had been isolated, was surrounded by people, and the showman—Michael Keenan—was shouting to them.

'Be patient, good people! I will certainly sell you some of my elephant remedy. But first I must put the elephant in here.'

A heavy foot thudded on to the ramp. Peering through a gap in the hay bales, Tad saw an enormous black shape blocking the doorway. It took one step towards him and then hesitated, flapping its ears.

'Move up, Khush!' Michael Keenan said, impatiently. Tad saw the silhouette of his short, sharp stick. 'Move up!'

The elephant still hesitated and the stick moved sideways, jabbing at the great flank. With a disapproving rumble, Khush rattled up the ramp and into the car.

The next moment, the ramp clanged up, shutting out most of the light. Tad heard a lock click and then the shuffling hum of the crowd moving back towards the depot.

He was locked in with the elephant.

The smell of it filled his nostrils and its movements rustled the hay that surrounded him. If he tried to call for help, who knew what it would do?

Tad cowered in the hay, trying not to breathe. But the elephant was tugging at the bales and reaching round them with its trunk. He couldn't see it, but he felt the bales shift and he muttered automatically, as if he were talking to a nervy horse.

'Steady, there. Steady, Khush.'

In answer, the long grey trunk snaked round the nearest bale and found his head. The delicate fingertip at the end of the trunk moved slowly over his face, from top to bottom and then from side to side, feeling the shape of his nose and the curve of his mouth.

It was damp and gentle. Gentler than any human hand Tad could remember. It brushed his closed eyelids, and a strange rumbling came from the elephant's stomach, low and soothing, like the purring of a contented cat. Tad kept absolutely still, barely breathing.

A second later, Khush turned away and began to pull at the hay, stuffing it into his mouth and reaching for more. He was like a huge wall between Tad and the door, immovable until Michael Keenan came back. Perhaps it was best to wait for that. Tad settled himself in his corner and let his eyes grow accustomed to the darkness.

But Michael Keenan was a long time. The hum of voices round the depot went on and on, and the air inside the wagon grew hotter as the sun got up. Slowly, lulled by the elephant's steady chewing, Tad let his eyelids close.

By the time the showman returned, he was fast asleep, curled up in the hay. And there was no noise from the door to wake him. Michael Keenan didn't open it. He simply peered through the slats and called to the elephant.

'Steady there, Khush. We're on our way now. Steady, boy.'

It was the crash of the metal that woke Tad, as the wagon was coupled on to the freight train. And by then it was too late. Khush shuffled and stamped and trumpeted as the car was hauled out of the siding, and no one heard Tad yelling and knocking on the side.

There was a long whistle and a jerk, and then the locomotive took up the slack, pulling the train out of the depot and away down the Tamaquon Valley.

After fifteen years of being watched and picked on and pointed at, Tad Hawkins slid out of Markle so secretly that no one, except an elephant, knew he had gone.

13

To Fru Kerstin Svensson,
Albery,
Nebraska.

Dearest Ketty,

You must forgive the shakiness of my handwriting. It is
partly due to the motion of the train, but more—much
more—to the sheer relief of finding myself sitting in this
seat, speeding safely away from Markle, Pennsylvania.

Today, Pa pulled the cripple scam again.

You see what happens when you are not here? It is not
eighteen months since he promised you, at your
wedding, that he would abandon it. But this morning I
was up in the air, showing the world the ribbons on my
drawers. And *terrified*, every second, that some busybody
would guess what was going on.

Fortunately, no one did. In all that crowd of
Dutchmen and miners, there was not a soul who
suspected.

They were on my side, before ever Khush came near
me. As I was standing in the crowd, a great, rough boy
(*twice* my size) came charging through to the front and
sent me flying. It was as good as an opera to see his face,
when he noticed the 'poor cripple' he had barged into.
Utterly crestfallen. And I—poor, dear, *fragile* little
thing— was the darling of the old ladies, from that
moment onwards.

As a result, Pa sold *four hundred* bottles of his precious
tincture and strutted on to the train like a new-made
congressman. They cheered him out of Markle. And
they cheered Olivia and me, as we passed. (Sitting, of
course, in a different carriage, and pretending that we
hardly knew Pa.)

I cheered too. And laughed and waved. I know I should not have done. I know it is wicked of Pa, to cheat such poor folk, and take their dollars. But they are so *stupid*, Ketty! Like the boy who bumped into me in the crowd. I think they cannot have brains, as we do.

Anyway, now we are safe. And we are leaving this horrible, dirty Tamaquon Valley and heading for the mountains—*to travel west!*

Not as far west as you, of course. Pa could not live at such a distance from a decent tailor, and he will not believe that there is human life west of the Mississippi. But we *are* crossing the Alleghenies, to try our luck in Pittsburgh. We are to pass tonight and tomorrow in Ginder Falls (in separate hotels, of course!) and then travel to Harrisburg, to catch a train over the mountains.

Oh, if only it were going all the way to Nebraska!

Dear Ketty, nothing is the same without you. No one brushes my hair *properly*, or cooks an apple pie worth eating. It is ridiculous of Hjalmar to keep you out there on the prairie when we need you so much.

Pa has no one to keep his notions in check, and Olivia has become overbearing. From playing my Mama, she fancies herself more than a mere sister, and orders me about even when we are alone. She would not dare to behave so if you were here.

And she shall not do it, even though you are gone! I shall speak to Pa about her, this very evening. He told us to keep away from him until we are over the Alleghenies, in case anyone from Markle should see us. But I shall find him this very night, when we reach Ginder Falls. I shall insist that he reprimands Olivia.

And then I shall continue this letter and tell you what he said.

CHAPTER 3

TAD GAVE up shouting at last, and slept again. When he woke the next time, they had been travelling for a long while. Khush's great heap of food had shrunk by half, and the sawdust on the floor was wet and foul.

He sat and listened to the elephant's slow movements, staring through the slats of the wagon at the valley rushing by. How was he going to get home? If they didn't stop before Ginder Falls, he would have to walk all the way back up the valley. Should he look for work in Ginder Falls first, to try and earn money for a railroad ticket?

Or perhaps Mr Keenan would help him.

But there was never any chance of that. As soon as they reached Ginder Falls, Michael Keenan came to unfasten the wagon. He lowered the ramp, saw Tad standing apologetically by Khush's head—and exploded. Racing down the wagon, in three huge strides, he caught Tad by the collar, choking the life out of him.

'If you've harmed a hair of that elephant's head, I'll roast you for breakfast, so help me! I'll fry you in pig's lard and seethe you in dripping! I'll—'

Tad spluttered and gasped, but he couldn't say a word.

'That elephant, *miserable* boy, is worth FIVE THOUSAND DOLLARS! Brought from India by sailing ship! Hand-reared by a Sikh elephant trainer! Lovingly nurtured by me—'

His voice boomed. What had been flamboyant in the depot at Markle was overpowering in the close, dark wagon. Even when he loosened his grip, Tad did not dare to speak.

But that made it worse. Michael Keenan snorted with rage and began to shake him, jerking his neck and clattering his teeth.

'Haven't you got a word to say for yourself? You miserable, sneaking, conniving—'

16

And then the elephant moved. His trunk shot forward, snatched Michael Keenan's tall hat off his head and lifted it high in the air. Then, with a flourish, it dropped the hat neatly on to Tad's head.

The terrible shaking stopped abruptly.

'Well, will you look at that now?' Michael Keenan stepped back and stared, first at Khush and then at Tad. 'I've never seen the creature behave like that. Did you see the snub he gave me? What have you been telling him?'

'I haven't—' Tad held out the hat. 'It was a mistake. I got trapped—'

Michael Keenan grinned, waved the hat in the air and dropped it back on to his own head. 'Could have been the last mistake of your life, boy. Khush doesn't usually fancy travelling companions. But all's well that ends well. And you've a fine tale to tell your grandchildren.'

He planted a hand in the middle of Tad's back and steered him down the wagon, towards the door. They were almost there, when someone came running up the ramp.

'Are you in there, Pa?'

Tad couldn't see anything except a dark shape in the doorway, but the voice seemed familiar. A girl's voice. Before he could work out who it was, Michael Keenan pushed him away, back into the wagon.

'Get out of here!' he snapped at the figure on the ramp.

'But I want to ask you—'

'Out!'

She took a step backwards and the light fell full on to her. Peering round Michael Keenan's shoulder, Tad saw a narrow, fragile face, framed by neat golden ringlets. The unmistakable face of the cripple girl from Markle depot.

He gasped. 'Pa?'

'Shut your mouth, now!' Michael Keenan slammed him sideways, into a corner of the wagon. His face loomed close and furious.

'If you've any idea of blabbing—'

'That's no use, Pa,' Cissie said scornfully. She came into

17

the wagon, picking her way over the dirty straw. 'Remember that boy at Harpers Ferry? He swore, all ways up, that he'd hold his tongue, but he got us run out of town, all the same.'

'A pity you couldn't hold *your* tongue,' Michael Keenan growled. 'I told you to keep away from me—'

'But I *can't endure* Olivia's airs—'

Cissie's fists were clenched and her ringlets shook with fury as she squared up to her father. Tad knew he should try to slip past, while they were quarrelling, but he dithered too long. Before he took a step, the two of them had turned on him again, glaring.

'He's *bound* to talk,' Cissie said. 'Unless we wrap him up in a parcel and take him with us.'

'I won't,' Tad said earnestly. 'I promise—'

'You don't really mean that. Of course you will—'

'Be quiet!' Michael Keenan shouted, at both of them. 'I want to think!' He was looking Tad up and down, and there was a strange gleam in his eyes. 'Not a parcel, but maybe . . . '

Cissie groaned. 'Pa! This is no time for one of your notions. We've got to be sensible.'

Her father waved a hand at her, without taking his eyes off Tad. 'Get back to Olivia. I can't think what she's about, letting you wander round a place like this on your own.'

'But I can't just leave you—'

'*Away!*'

Cissie pouted, but she went.

The shouting had disturbed Khush. He was shifting from foot to foot and rattling his trunk restlessly against the floor of the wagon. Michael Keenan put an arm round Tad's shoulders and drew him down the ramp.

'Best leave the creature to settle down, while we two have a chat.' He smiled jovially. 'Who do you live with, boy? Mother and father? Are they scouring the country for their lost little darling?'

'They're dead,' Tad said. 'I live with my aunt, in Markle.'

Michael Keenan's eyes brightened. 'And you are the apple of her eye, no doubt? The ray of sunshine to light her declining years?'

'She's very good to me.'

Tad meant to sound humble and grateful, but the words came out like icicles. Michael Keenan bellowed with laughter and clapped him on the back.

'I know the kind of woman. Does you one kindness and makes you say thank you a thousand times.' He beamed at Tad's reluctant grin. 'You're just the boy I've been looking for. I need someone to travel with Khush and do the rough work.'

'To travel—' Tad's head spun. 'But I don't know anything about elephants.'

'You will, if you travel with me! I'll turn you into the finest elephant handler in the country.'

'I—' Tad didn't know how to start thinking about it. He'd never expected to leave Markle. Never thought of anything beyond doing Aunt Adah's chores and being shouted at.

But Michael Keenan didn't wait for an answer. He strode up and down, his coat flapping open with a dazzle of scarlet silk.

'We could work two elephants. Three, even! That would set everyone talking! We could travel the country, from here to the Mississippi.'

Tad hardly knew what the Mississippi was, let alone where it might be. And he was not sure that he trusted Michael Keenan. He edged away from the elephant wagon.

'I don't think I'm the person you want.'

Michael Keenan whirled round and gave him a broad, open smile. 'And why not? Do you think I might stick a knife in your back one day? And drop you in the nearest creek, to keep my secrets safe?' He chuckled as Tad looked down at his feet. 'What would your friend the elephant say if I did? He'd smell your blood on my hands.'

That didn't sound very likely. Tad edged further away, and Michael Keenan gave a charming grin. Charming, but with an edge as sharp as steel.

'You've nothing to fear. But I can't let you go home, to blab my business everywhere. And by the sound of it, you've nothing to go home for. We have to fall in together, boy.'

There didn't seem to be any way of saying no. Twenty

minutes later, Tad was standing in the railyard, learning how to scrub an elephant.

'I want it done every day,' Michael Keenan said briskly. 'Or we'll have a sick, unsavoury animal. You can start now.'

Tad looked down at the scrubbing broom in his hands. Then he looked up, at the great grey slab that was Khush's side. 'Maybe you should show me—'

'There's nothing to it, boy. Keep a good eye to the animal and give me a call when you're done.' With a cheerful nod, Michael Keenan swaggered off to the depot and Tad was alone with the elephant and the scrubbing broom.

He swallowed. Aunt Adah wouldn't even trust him to wash her best china. Now here he was, in charge of five thousand dollars' worth of elephant. He might hurt it. Or it might hurt *him*. Or snap its chain and run off into the town. Or—

But he had to do something. There was a crowd of children gathering, and Khush was staring down expectantly. Slowly, Tad dipped the broom into the bucket of water. Maybe it wouldn't be so daunting if he pretended that those grey, weathered flanks were stone flags, like the ones in Aunt Adah's wash-house.

He began nervously, but the broom had a reassuring feel. He did know how to scrub, after all. He'd done plenty of that. Gradually, the familiar rhythm took over and, without realizing it, he began to whistle as he worked.

Half an hour later, with a crowd of people watching, he put down the broom and turned to see Michael Keenan close behind. He was grinning as he came forward.

'You've made a fine job of it!'

'I hope I've got him clean enough—'

'Couldn't be cleaner! I've had an eye on you all the time, and I've never seen an elephant better scrubbed. Well done!'

The words floated in the air and, for a moment, Tad had to breathe harder, to stop himself feeling dizzy. It was the first time he had ever been praised for doing something right.

CHAPTER 4

AFTERWARDS, TAD wondered why he hadn't run away in that first week. It would have been easy enough. But something kept him travelling with Michael Keenan—even when they reached a safe distance from Markle, and he worked the cripple trick again.

Praise was one of the things Tad stayed for. He heard more in that week than in all the rest of his life. Every day, he washed Khush and cleaned out the wagon and carried in fresh food and water. And every day, Michael Keenan rewarded him with extravagant, enthusiastic praise.

'You never need telling twice! And you've a wonderful way with Khush. You might have been trained as an elephant boy!'

Tad grinned at that, wondering what Aunt Adah would have said, but it was true. He knew all about mops and scrubbing brushes and hot water. And he soon got used to working round an elephant. Cleaning up after Khush was no worse than fighting the coal dust in Markle.

The other thing that held him was the hope of being paid. Nothing had been said about money, but he wanted to earn his fare back to Markle. Could Michael Keenan afford that?

It was difficult to tell. They were working their way to Harrisburg, travelling as quietly as they could. After that second appearance, Cissie's crutches had been packed away in the wagon, with the wonderful green tincture. There would be no miraculous cures now until they were over the mountains, where people had never heard of them.

But every day Khush earned money by giving rides. Cissie and Olivia stayed in the best hotel in every town and whenever Tad glimpsed them out walking they were wearing fine, fashionable clothes.

There was money for Michael Keenan to jingle in his

pocket, too. Every evening, wherever they were, he set off to look for a card game, and he never came back until long after midnight.

But it was harder to find money to pay the daily bill for Khush's food, and there was never a word about wages for Tad.

When they reached Harrisburg, he decided that he had to ask. Once they were over the mountains, he might not be needed any more. Without wages, he would be stranded. He stood in the railyard that evening, waiting for Michael Keenan to bring Khush back and planning what he would say. His hands shook as he imagined the conversation, but he knew that he had to ask.

At the first sound of footsteps behind him, he whirled round nervously. But it wasn't Mr Keenan. It was a man and a woman, walking across the yard. A broad, heavy man and a thin woman who clung on to his arm. Tad was about to look away again when the woman spoke, calling across the space between them.

'Tad? Is that Tad? What are *you* doing here?'

The voice was sharp and familiar. Tad dropped the pitchfork with a clatter and caught his breath. Surely it was impossible?

The man shook his arm free and walked across the railyard towards Tad. When he was close he nodded.

'I didn't think you had the wits to get so far.'

Tad shuddered at the thick, oily voice. 'Mr Jackson?'

There was no mistaking the voice, and the ponderous walk. Tad glanced at the woman, who was picking her way over the tracks. The flounced dress and the purple bonnet feathers were strange, but he knew who it was now. Only Esther tossed her head in that brisk, sulky way.

But what was she doing in Harrisburg? With Mr Jackson?

She didn't explain. As soon as she was near, she wrinkled her nose and frowned.

'What in the world have you been doing? You smell as though you've been mucking out a cow byre.'

'It was an elephant wagon,' Tad said stiffly.

22

Esther sniffed. 'I wouldn't let you near any wagon of mine. Nor anything else I owned.'

Tad shrugged and turned away, but as he did so he knocked the handle of the pitchfork. It fell on to the muddy ground, spattering dirt on Esther's flounces.

'You see?' She shook the flounces angrily. 'Are you telling me Mr Keenan's given you a *job*?'

'Now then. No point in riling the boy.'

Mr Jackson put his arm round her waist and squeezed, but that didn't please her either. She pushed the arm away and glared at Tad.

'Don't you go thinking things, just because we're here together. Mr Jackson and I have got a business partnership.'

'Indeed we have,' Mr Jackson said smoothly. He replaced his arm and squeezed again with a defiant nod, daring Tad to make something of it. 'We've been following your Mr Keenan. Keeping an eye on him. And we think it's time he had a quiet word with us. Is he anywhere about?'

'I—he—' Tad stuttered stupidly, trying not to watch as Mr Jackson's fingers slid up into Esther's hair and pulled at her earlobe.

'The boy's a halfwit!' Esther shook her head free and pointed. 'There's Mr Keenan now, bringing the elephant back.'

Tad was being trained to handle Khush and normally he would have run across to take charge of him. But he hung back. He couldn't imagine giving orders in front of Father. Or Mr Jackson.

It was Mr Jackson who walked across the yard, with his hand held out. By the time he met Michael Keenan, he was out of earshot, but Tad saw him grab the showman's hand and shake it vigorously. Esther set off towards them and Tad turned away and went on pitching hay into the wagon. If they had business together, it was better to leave them alone.

But he had only pitched half a dozen forkfuls when there was a loud, angry shout.

'Tad! Where are you, boy? I don't pay you to stand about!'

You don't pay me at all, thought Tad, but that wasn't the

23

moment to say it. He ran across the yard. Esther was standing with her hands folded, watching the two men as they faced each other. Michael Keenan was wild-eyed and furious, his tall hat tilted back on his head and his face flushed, but Mr Jackson was calm.

'You'd be sensible to think it over,' he said, as Tad came up to them. His voice was soft, but ominous. 'I've offered you a fair price.'

'Call that a fair price?' Michael Keenan bellowed. 'Five hundred dollars? It's an insult, so it is!'

'Ah, but it's not just the money we're offering,' Esther said slyly. 'It's our silence, as well. You can't afford to say no.'

'I'll say no whenever I like, to damned blackmail!'

'That's no language to use to a lady.' Mr Jackson reached out and grabbed Michael Keenan's lapel. For the first time, Tad realized what strength there was in those fat, clammy fingers. 'You can apologize, right now.'

'Apologize be—'

Khush didn't like the shouting. He rumbled irritably, and that provoked another shout.

'Tad? What's taking you so long? Get this creature out of here!'

'I—sorry.'

'And stop saying you're sorry, or I'll glue up your tongue!'

Tad reached out to take the bullhook, dropped it and fumbled to pick it up. Then he muttered the order.

'Move up, Khush.'

'What makes you think he'll take any notice of that?' Michael Keenan rolled his eyes dramatically up to heaven. 'Say it as though you mean it!'

Tad saw Esther smirk and he stuttered the order again. 'M-move up.'

It didn't sound any better, but Khush started to lumber towards the wagon. As Tad followed, he heard Mr Jackson's voice again.

'We won't take no for an answer. I hear you're going to Pittsburgh tomorrow morning? Well, Miss Lanigan and I will be on the train.'

24

Then Tad was too far away to catch any more. But as he followed Khush he wondered what Mr Jackson wanted. And why Mr Keenan did not send him packing.

He got a kind of answer half an hour later, when Michael Keenan came clattering into the wagon.

'Get yourself ready now, boy. We're leaving this evening.'

'I thought it was tomorrow.'

'And so it was. But not with those two following us. We can't afford regular customers in our business. They get to know a deal too much. We'll sneak off today, and give them the slip.'

He sounded very confident, but Tad wondered why. If Mr Jackson had any sense, he would be keeping a watch on the freight yard. Even in the dark, it would be easy to see if the big, red elephant-wagon moved.

But Michael Keenan had no caution in his nature. As if the elephant-wagon weren't eye-catching enough, he came to see it off himself. Until the very last moment, he was standing close beside it, whispering instructions through the slats to Tad.

'I'll be on the train half an hour behind, with Olivia and Cissie. Open the wagon doors at Pittsburgh if you need fresh air, but keep the animal inside until I come.'

Tad thought he would have plenty of air without that. A strong, cold wind was rising, whistling between the slats and blowing in sharp, powerful gusts round his shoulders. But he nodded obediently.

Then he put his eye to a gap and watched as they slipped away out of the depot. Michael Keenan was standing with his hands on his hips and his head flung back, gazing after them. His tall hat gleamed in the lamplight and the lining of his coat glowed rich, brilliant red as the wind blew it open.

It was the last time that Tad ever saw him.

In care of Mrs P. Alexander,
Pittsburgh
10th April

I said I would continue this letter when I had spoken to
Pa, but he would not let me near him. And now—

Dearest Ketty, I hope you may have seen a newspaper
from the east before you receive this, so that I am not the
first to break the terrible news to you.

If you do not know what I mean, gather all your
strength before you read on.

My dear father and my dear sister Olivia were killed
yesterday in a railroad accident which destroyed the
entire fabric of two cars of the train. They were derailed
by a fallen tree and, when their stoves overturned,
caught fire instantly, causing great loss of life.

I owe my own preservation to the fact that my seat was
beside a window. By the mercy of God, I was flung out
and suffered no greater harm than cuts and bruises.

I was brought to this house by an official of the
railroad company. Mrs Alexander is good enough to say
that I may lodge here until my relatives come to claim
me.

But I have no relatives now. (Even if I could find my
mother, I should not recognize her after so many years.)
All I have in the world is the elephant. If no one claims
me, he will be sold, and the money used to board me out
with Mrs Alexander, or some other person, while I learn
a trade.

Dear Ketty, please do not leave me here to become a
milliner or a laundress. If Hjalmar will let me come to
live with you, I will sell Khush and give the money to
you. You can have it all, if you will only let me come—

CHAPTER 5

THE FREIGHT train had arrived on time, early in the morning. From the moment it pulled into the depot, Khush was irritable, stamping his feet and tossing hay around. Tad murmured soothing words for a while, but they didn't seem to work, and he was stiff and cold from hours of sitting in the draughty wagon.

He lowered the ramp and looked out at the dirty sky. Falling drizzle and rising smoke blew in the wild, grey canopy over Pittsburgh, muffling all the buildings.

Pittsburgh! Michael Keenan had said grandly. *The great junction of the Allegheny and the Monongahela! The key to the Ohio!* But Tad couldn't see any rivers, only roofs and railroad tracks. He picked up a bucket and let himself out of the wagon.

'Steady there, Khush,' he muttered. 'Time to fetch some fresh water.' Swinging the bucket, he went towards the nearest railroad buildings.

Fifty yards away, he knew that something terrible had happened. Half a dozen men were huddled together with solemn faces and as he got closer he heard what they were saying.

' . . . more than fifty dead . . . driver too . . . they say it's still blazing . . . '

Tad gripped the handle of his bucket.

'The—the train from Harrisburg—?'

He did not realize that he had spoken aloud until the men turned round. When they did, he didn't need any other answer. He gripped the bucket even harder.

'I—I was waiting for Mr Keenan. The—the elephant—' Stuttering, he pointed back at the bright red wagon with the gold lettering.

He meant to ask them for news. To try and discover what

had happened. But as soon as he said *elephant*, the men started to hustle him back towards the wagon.

' . . . better keep the creature happy . . . '

'We'll find out what we can . . . '

'Need water? Hay?'

' . . . we'll send someone . . . '

Stumbling across the yard, Tad climbed into the wagon, without really knowing what he was doing. His brain was boiling, and hectic pictures danced behind his eyes. Michael Keenan, with his scarlet lining flapping. Olivia, very tall and slim in her brown cloth dress. And Cissie—

He tried hard not to think about Cissie.

Something damp and gentle touched his earlobe. He looked up and saw that it was the tip of Khush's trunk. For a second he brushed his hand over the thick, rough skin.

Then he picked up the broom and unfastened Khush's chain, to lead him out of the wagon. 'Move up there! No reason to stay dirty.'

Clumsily at first, with a lot of splashing, he began the familiar routine of scrubbing. After ten minutes he was thinking more clearly, putting his ideas in order to the rhythm of the brush strokes.

Michael Keenan didn't have to be dead. Fifty people were killed, but there must be dozens—hundreds, maybe—left alive. The crash must have thrown everything into confusion, but once that was sorted out Michael Keenan would surely come walking into the yard with his hat on a tilt and his coat flapping. Surely.

Tad waited.

The drizzle thickened and the savage wind dropped as the day wore on, but there was no news. The people who drifted by to stare at Khush had nothing fresh to tell Tad. And he did not dare to go off on his own and find out more, because Khush was jumpy and badtempered, staring through the slats as though he expected someone.

Tad walked him round the yard, for exercise, but when the sun went down the evening turned chilly. He had to lead Khush back into the shelter of the wagon and chain him up.

He was just wondering whether to lift the ramp and bolt it when someone called across the yard.

'Hey! Boy! The man's here, asking for his elephant!'

The man—

Tad gasped, caught his breath and ran. Tripping on the sleepers and blundering into huge wheels in the dark, he threw himself across the tracks towards the voices, grinning idiotically.

'I knew it!' he called. 'I *knew* you were all right—'

And then he saw who was standing in the light of the lantern. A heavy middle-aged man with bloodshot eyes, and a sharp-faced young woman who hung on his arm.

The clerk grinned cheerfully. 'Can you take them across, boy?'

'B-but he's not—they're not—'

'Not what?' Mr Jackson said. In the lantern-light, his face was like a great slab of rock, cut by deep grooves. 'Not the owner?' He smiled slowly, but the grooves did not alter. 'You've got it wrong, Tad. I bought that elephant last night.'

Tad stared. 'But you can't—'

'For heaven's sake!' Esther's fingers rippled impatiently on Mr Jackson's arm. 'Show him the paper, Hannibal. It's too cold to stand here arguing.'

Mr Jackson took a folded paper from his pocket and spread it out for Tad to see. 'Mr Keenan and I had a long, long talk on the train. He saw the sense in what I was saying and we struck a deal before we'd crossed the Alleghenies.'

He held the paper under the lantern, running a fleshy finger along the lines, and the words seemed to jump out at Tad.

It was a receipt for five hundred dollars, paid to Mr Michael Keenan, in return for which, Mr Keenan handed over to Mr Hannibal Jackson all his rights in the male Indian elephant known as Khush, together with the travelling vehicle and all implements necessary for the care of the said elephant.

Five *hundred* dollars? Tad read it again and then looked up. 'But I can't just hand over—Where's Mr Keenan?'

Mr Jackson took back the receipt and folded it carefully, smoothing the creases. 'Miss Lanigan and I left him in the

29

front car, after he'd signed the paper. We went to the back of the train—and that was our good fortune. When we crashed, the front two cars went up in flames.'

He said it without emotion, not even looking up. Everything in Tad's head went very still. 'And Mr Keenan?'

The railroad clerk put a hand on his shoulder. 'No one was saved from those cars. Only one little girl.'

'The poor little cripple that was cured in Markle.' Esther's eyes opened very wide, in elaborate innocence. 'Just fancy— she turned out to be Mr Keenan's daughter!'

'Cissie?' That was something solid, in the middle of all the confusion. 'Cissie's alive? But then the elephant—'

'The elephant belongs to me,' Mr Jackson said calmly.

'Of course it does!' Esther snapped. 'That girl has nothing to do with it!' Then she remembered the railroad clerk and twisted her face into a sentimental smile. 'The poor little thing's got too much on her mind to be worrying about elephants.'

'But I must tell her,' Tad said. He couldn't just give Khush to Mr Jackson. Someone had to tell him it was all fair and legal. Maybe Cissie could. 'Where is she?'

'She's boarded out safely, until her relations come,' Mr Jackson said. 'It's not my business to know where. Maybe someone in the railroad office can tell you.' He glanced at the clerk, who nodded.

'I must find out, then—'

'Not tonight. You can track her down in the morning, if you must. Tonight I have to get the elephant out of this yard, and you will have to help me. Just for the time being.'

'The time being?' Tad repeated, not understanding.

Esther snorted. 'You can't be expecting us to give you a job? Don't forget, I know all about you. We just need you for the next couple of days.'

'It won't take me long to get the measure of the animal,' Mr Jackson said smoothly. 'But I must learn the right commands. I've found a livery stable where he can stay, and they'll let you sleep there.'

It all seemed rushed and peculiar and uncertain. Tad looked

across at the elephant-wagon and then back at Mr Jackson.

'I don't know whether I should.'

'It's not for you to know anything.' Mr Jackson reached out to take the lantern from the railway clerk and then grabbed Tad's arm, digging his fingers in. 'The elephant is mine. And anyone who tries to cheat me out of what is mine will have the law to reckon with.'

He held the lantern high. For a second he and Tad faced each other in the pool of light, and Tad looked full into his cold eyes and shuddered.

Then Esther came up on his other side, so close that her feathers brushed against Tad's face. 'Hannibal always gets what he wants,' she said triumphantly. 'He's wanted that elephant since the moment he saw it, and now he's got it— and we're going to make our fortunes!'

The two of them began to lead Tad across the yard, towards the wagon. When they reached it, Mr Jackson held the lantern high and stared into the shadows inside.

'That animal is wasted in the east,' he said softly. 'People are spoilt for entertainment here. But out west, in the cattle towns and the mining towns, there's nothing for a man to spend his money on. I can show the elephant, and give rides, and take bets—men will bet on anything there, out of sheer boredom!'

He took a deep breath and waved the lantern.

'Bring it out, boy. Let's take a look at it.'

Tad stumbled up the ramp and undid Khush's chain, his fingers slipping on the cold metal. Then he led the elephant out.

'Move up there. Move up, Khush.'

Obediently, Khush shuffled down the ramp, and Esther sniffed.

'If Tad can order the animal around like that, it shouldn't take you more than a couple of days to learn.'

Mr Jackson nodded, without looking at her. He was staring at Khush. 'A goldmine on four legs!' he murmured. 'A man couldn't fail, with a creature like that.'

Esther slipped her hand through his arm and squeezed it, but Tad turned away from his greedy, gloating smile.

CHAPTER 6

IT WAS almost dark by the time they reached the livery stables. The owner found Khush a grudging place in the back yard, behind the main buildings.

'I want him kept out here,' he said, as he pocketed Mr Jackson's money. 'Chained up. Can't have him spooking the horses.'

'You hear that?' Esther pinched Tad's arm. 'He's not to come off the chain.' Straightening her purple feathers, she smiled graciously at the stable man. 'Don't you worry, Mr Presswood. Tad will keep him in order.'

The man grunted. 'Get the boy to sleep in the shed there.' He pointed to a hovel in one corner of the yard. 'I'm not taking responsibility. Someone has to be here all the time.'

He moved off, and Esther pinched Tad again. 'You hear that? Don't you dare move out of the yard. We don't want any trouble.'

'All right,' Tad mumbled.

Esther tossed her head. 'All right *what?*'

Tad stared. Then swallowed. 'All right, *ma'am.*'

Mr Jackson smiled and Esther slipped her hand through his arm. They swept out, leaving Tad to make Khush as comfortable as he could.

It wasn't easy. The yard was hard and damp, and there was no shelter big enough for an elephant. Tad found a rusty ring, let into the ramshackle wall that ran round three sides of the yard and he attached Khush's leg chain to that. Then he fetched water, to fill the cracked, slimy trough, and scrounged as much straw as he could for Khush to lie on.

The elephant's small, patient eyes watched him as he scurried round with the lantern. And behind Khush, first to one side and then to the other, danced his gigantic shadow, swelling and dwindling over the dirty yard.

There was nothing Tad could do about the horses, once they caught the smell of elephant. All night long, the air was full of stamping hoofs and nervous whinnying. And the dogs tugged at their chains and yapped round the gate that led from the stables to the back yard.

When Mr Jackson came in the next morning, he was frowning.

'That elephant won't be welcome here for long. You'd better teach me all the commands today. Then I can move on tomorrow.'

Tad blinked. 'I was only with Mr Keenan for a week. I can't tell you much.'

'You'll have to do the best you can.' Mr Jackson ran his eyes over Khush. 'One dumb creature is much like another.'

'I don't think—'

'No one's asking you to think. Just tell me what you do first.'

Tad showed him how to scrub. It took three times as long as usual, because Khush was jumpy and irritable. Every time footsteps came near the gate he turned to see who was coming, and when Mr Jackson took a turn with the scrubbing broom he wrenched it away with his trunk and flung it across the yard.

Mr Jackson's eyes narrowed. 'That animal needs to be taught a lesson. What have you got to keep it under control? Give me that jabbing stick.'

He picked up the bullhook and held it very still, in front of Khush's face.

'Give him a chance,' Tad said. 'He doesn't know what's happened. He's waiting for—'

'There's no point in waiting for a dead man. I'm its master now and it has to learn. Tell me how to make it walk.'

Tad taught him a few simple commands and he practised them, accompanying each one with a jab from the bullhook. By the time Esther appeared in the yard, Khush was shuffling round sulkily whenever he was told.

Esther beamed. 'There you are. I told you it was easy. We don't need Tad.'

Tad wondered which of them was going to scrub out the wagon and fetch fifty gallons of water every day. But he didn't ask. Instead, he said, 'Can I go, then?'

Mr Jackson looked at him. 'Go?'

'I ought to find Mr Keenan's daughter. I was left in charge of the elephant. It doesn't seem right to hand him over without telling her.'

There was a small pause. Then Mr Jackson nodded. 'Be back this evening, to stay with the elephant. And tomorrow, to help me load it into its wagon. Make yourself useful, and there'll be a dollar for you when we go.'

'I'll be there,' Tad said.

He turned to leave, but Mr Jackson stopped him, holding out a hand.

'The key,' he said.

Reluctantly, Tad handed over the key to the chain. Then he headed for the back gate, to avoid going through the main stable yard. Khush's eyes followed him and he turned, with his hand on the gate.

'Steady, then. I'll be back soon.'

Khush rumbled protestingly, and Tad felt a small shiver of guilt as he walked through into the alley. But there was no help for it. He had to make sure Cissie knew what was happening.

Pittsburgh was far bigger than Markle. Bigger than anywhere Tad had ever dreamt of. The livery stable was out on the east side of town and he lost himself three times on the way to the railroad depot. Wherever he turned, he seemed to hit a river bank.

Without help, he would never have found the house where Cissie was staying, but the men in the office were sympathetic.

'That poor little waif with the big eyes? I reckon she needs to see a friendly face. Wait ten minutes, and Pat can set you on the way.'

Pat did better than that. He took Tad right to the house

34

and introduced him to the suspicious woman who opened the door.

'You'll forgive the state of his clothes, Mrs Alexander. It's all on account of the elephant.'

Mrs Alexander sniffed, as though nothing in the world could excuse the state of Tad's clothes, but she let him in and showed him to the parlour.

'If you ask me,' she said sourly, 'that elephant ought to be sold. The girl hasn't got a cent to her name, and I can't keep her for ever.'

With another sniff, she went off down the corridor, and Tad knocked on the parlour door.

'Miss Cissie?'

He didn't know what to expect. Tears? Hysterical shrieks? Fainting? He knew that females were inclined to be emotional. Especially young females.

But Cissie wasn't shrieking or crying. She was sitting at the bureau in the corner of the parlour, writing feverishly. When Tad walked in, she jumped up and pushed the paper into her pocket.

'It's you! Is Khush all right? You know what's happened?'

Tad nodded awkwardly. She looked even smaller than he remembered, and very pale and hectic. 'I'm sorry—'

'We won't talk about that. *If* you please.' Cissie pushed her hands into her sleeves and began to walk briskly up and down the little parlour, taking three steps one way, turning, and taking three steps back. 'I shall be just fine. When I can go to my friend's.'

'Your friend?' That was unexpected. Tad had imagined her all alone in the world.

Cissie stopped walking and began to rearrange the ornaments on the mantelshelf, twitching at the plush fringe that hung down in front. 'My friend Kerstin Gilstring—Kerstin Svensson—who used to travel with us. Until she got married.'

'She'll take you in?'

'Of course she will! She was like a mother to me. She'll tell me to come right away. The moment she gets my letter.'

Cissie patted the pocket with the paper in. Then she

35

walked restlessly back across the room and began to straighten the folds of the curtain.

So it was all right! Tad felt a weight lifting off him. If Cissie was going to live with a married friend, she wouldn't have any use for an elephant. 'It's worked out well, then. With Khush.'

'Worked out well?' Cissie whirled round, frowning.

'You wouldn't be able to take him. Not to your friend's. Your Pa sold him just at the right time.'

'*Sold* him?' Cissie stopped fidgeting and her pale face turned sheet-white. 'What are you talking about? Pa didn't sell Khush.'

'On the train, miss.' Tad looked nervously at her. 'He sold him to Mr Jackson.'

'But that's nonsense!'

'I've seen the paper.'

Cissie stood rigid, staring at him. '*Sold Khush?*'

'And the wagon, miss. And everything to do with the elephant. Except for the bottles of tincture, maybe.'

'Oh, wonderful!' Cissie's mouth twisted bitterly. 'My fortune consists of ten dozen bottles of green tincture?'

She walked up the room and down again, without speaking. Then she began to rattle questions at Tad.

'How much money did Pa get for Khush? Tell me the exact words on the paper! What about the signature?'

Tad answered as best he could, and she snorted with scorn.

'Five *hundred* dollars? I've heard Pa say a dozen times that Khush was worth five thousand. And signed in black ink? Pa always wrote in blue. He said black was the mark of a commercial mind.'

'But, miss—'

Cissie's face was burning scarlet now. She grabbed Tad's arm and shook it. 'Don't you see? It's as plain as the nose on your face. The paper's a forgery!'

'A forgery?'

'Of course! They knew that Pa was dead, and couldn't deny his signature, so they forged it. To steal my elephant!'

'But I don't think—'

Cissie shook his arm again. 'Do you think my father would

have signed away the only valuable thing he owned, for such a pitiful sum of money?'

'He did refuse Mr Jackson before,' Tad said slowly. 'Said it was blackmail. Said five hundred dollars was an insult, and the elephant was worth five thousand.'

'You see?'

Cissie looked triumphant, and Tad drew a long, unhappy breath.

'You have to look at it like this, miss. Mr Jackson has a paper that seems all fair and legal. It's got your father's name at the bottom, with Esther—Miss Lanigan—as a witness—'

'Esther?' Cissie let go of his arm and looked at him sharply. 'You know these people?'

'Mr Jackson was my aunt's lodger,' Tad said, even more unhappily. 'And Esther was the hired help. But I'm not—'

Her face closed up, growing wooden with suspicion, and he began gabbling, to get her to understand.

'I didn't know what they were up to. I swear it! Why should I want Khush sold, when it means losing my job?'

Cissie clenched her fists. 'You expect me to believe that?'

'It's true!'

'Prove it then! Help me get back what's mine! I'm not going to wait around here and let Mr Jackson steal my elephant.'

She looked very determined, standing in front of him with her head flung back, but Tad could hardly believe that she was in earnest.

'You're going to *take* Khush?'

'That's right. And you're going to help me!'

If she had asked him, he would have argued. But she just gave the order, and he nodded, automatically.

'Good,' Cissie said. 'Now tell me where they're keeping him.'

By great good fortune, I was interrupted before I could take this to the post. Now, there is no time for more than the fastest few words.

I have to leave this place. I do not know where I shall be by tomorrow night, but I shall be with Khush. Enemies are trying to cheat me out of what is rightly mine, but do not worry. They will not succeed!

I shall set out tonight, to take him to a place where the thieves cannot find him. When we are safe, I shall write and tell you where we are, and then you *must* let me come to you.

I shall make sure that I have Khush, and you shall have every cent that he is worth!

CHAPTER 7

AT THE livery stable, Tad huddled uneasily in his rickety shed. Outside in the darkness, the dogs barked and the horses stamped and whinnied. He knew he should sleep, but his eyes refused to stay closed. His mind was churning miserably, full of Cissie's instructions.

Then, at midnight, he opened the door to check that Khush was all right and saw—nothing. Not even Khush, although he could hear him munching, very close. The yard was invisible. Fog had slid down on to Pittsburgh, writhing into every alley and narrow back yard and carrying the dry smell of coal smoke wherever it went.

Tad closed his eyes and leaned against the doorpost. He hadn't realized, until that moment, how much Cissie's plan had frightened him. But now the fog had made it impossible. He turned back into the shed, wriggled under some dusty straw and fell asleep.

Two hours later, Cissie woke him up. She crouched close to his face, holding a lantern over him as she shook his shoulder.

'Why are you asleep? I told you to be ready!'

'How did you ever—?' Tad blinked up at her. 'Has the fog cleared?'

'No, it hasn't. I had to follow the rivers to be sure of finding you. I've been all the way round the Point in the dark.'

Tad didn't know what she meant, but he could feel how cold she was. She picked up his boots and dropped them on top of him.

'Put these on! We have to get started!'

'But the fog—'

'The fog is wonderful! Better than anything we could have

39

planned. Come *on*!' She put down the lantern and tried to push his feet into his boots.

'But—'

'There's no time to argue!'

Tad pulled on the boots and crept after her, out into the yard. She threw her shawl over the lantern and they had to feel their way round the walls to where Khush was chained, moving towards the sound of his shuffling feet.

It was Tad who put his hand on the iron ring. Khush's chain ran through it, and both ends were locked to the metal anklet round his back leg. The links of the chain felt cold and damp under Tad's fingers.

And Mr Jackson had the key.

Cissie's hand met Tad's, running the other way up the chain, and he heard her sigh with relief.

'Only one leg chained. That's good. Hold on to the ring, and don't let it fall when it comes loose.'

In the main stable yard, the dogs caught the faint sound of her voice and threw themselves into a frenzy of barking. But Khush rumbled contentedly and scraped his feet over the cobbles.

'Steady there,' Cissie crooned, feeling her way along the chain towards him. 'Not yet.'

He rumbled again as she reached him, and she murmured very softly, so that Tad barely heard.

'Move up. Move up, there.'

The chain tautened and Khush strained at it for a moment. Then he let it go slack.

Cissie hissed more fiercely. 'Move up, Khush!'

This time he stayed quite still, except for a puzzled snort.

'I've got to get him moving,' Cissie whispered. 'Where's the bullhook?'

Tad fumbled back to the shed and found the short, thick stick with the steel tip. Cissie snatched it out of his hands and gestured back towards the ring. 'Don't let that drop. And watch yourself. He won't be pleased.'

Dimly, through the fog, Tad saw her swing the stick and jab forwards as she hissed her order again.

'Move *up*, Khush!'

There was a roar of rage that sent the dogs wild, and the chain jerked so hard that Tad felt the great iron ring shift in the wall.

Cissie jabbed again. 'Move up!'

This time, the roar was ear-splitting. Khush heaved with all his strength and the iron ring slid out of the wall with a grating noise that sounded like thunder.

Tad leapt forward and shook the ring under Cissie's nose. Immediately, she began to soothe Khush.

'Steady there. Well done. Steady.'

But there had been too much noise to ignore. The dogs were flinging themselves at the gate, barking frantically. The sleepy stable boys shouted uselessly for a moment. Then one of them kicked the dogs into silence and shuffled across the yard. The gate creaked open.

'What's going on? Where's Mr Jackson's boy?'

Tad held his breath. Cissie nudged him, but she couldn't tell him what to say.

'Hallo!' he called weakly.

'What's up with that elephant of yours?'

'He's—er—he's nervous. Misses Mr Keenan.'

The stable boy snorted. 'Then give him some of that medicine Mr Jackson was trying to sell us. Cures everything, by all accounts.'

'I'll—I'll try—'

Tad was hoping the stable boy would give up and go away. But Cissie, beside him, suddenly clenched her fists and began to shake with silent fury, and that set Khush off again, trumpeting and rattling his chain.

'Are you sure that elephant's all right?' the boy asked suspiciously. 'Maybe I ought to come and take a look.'

'You needn't bother,' Tad said. 'He's just—'

But he could hear the boy shuffling over the cobbles, muttering as he came closer.

'Where are you, you ugly creature? You can't be very— aargh!'

The last word vanished in a scream of terror, followed by

41

the noise of running feet. Thudding into the gate, the boy scrambled through and crashed it shut behind him. Tad could hear the others laughing as he gasped out his story.

'Creature caught me a wallop round the head with that trunk! It's a savage brute! *You* can go and see it, if you like, but I'm keeping away. I'm paid to look after horses, not wild animals.'

There was a roar of laughter, and more barking. Under cover of the noise, Cissie grabbed Tad's sleeve and whispered in his ear. *She* wasn't laughing.

'Did you hear? That man's even tried to steal my elephant tincture! Well, we're not leaving it for him. Have you got it in your hut?'

'We can't take that!' Tad said. The bottles were packed in two big, wooden boxes, roped together for slinging over Khush's back.

'They're *mine*. Go and get them!'

As Tad ducked into the hut, the face he pulled was hidden by the fog. He slipped the ropes over his shoulder and staggered out again with the boxes. For a moment, he couldn't work out where Cissie was. Then she called, from Khush's back.

'I'm up here! Pass them up.'

Tad heaved the first box high enough for Cissie to reach. She dropped it over Khush's neck and settled the second one in its place.

'Now follow!' she hissed. 'Carry the chain.'

With the rusty iron ring in his hand, Tad padded behind Khush, across the damp cobbles and through the rickety gate at the back of the yard. He had no idea where they were going, or what Cissie's plans were. He followed blindly.

'We'll keep by the river,' she whispered from above. 'That way we're sure to walk out of town, and not back into it.'

That sounded like a stop-gap plan, born of the fog. Tad felt uneasy, but arguing would have made too much noise. Even the sound of Khush's shuffling feet seemed deafening and he was certain that people would hear their voices if they kept talking. He kept his worries to himself and followed.

They edged along the alley and out towards the river. A fresh, muddy scent seeped towards them, mixing with the smell of coal, just as it did along the Tamaquon river, on the edge of Markle. Tad caught the familiar whisper of fast, high water rushing through tall plants.

A foot at a time, without seeing where they were going, they made their way out of Pittsburgh. Tad tried to imagine what would happen when daylight came and the fog cleared.

Mr Jackson would be after them, the second he missed Khush. And they wouldn't be hard to follow. They must have left footprints, and enough of a scent for a clever dog to trace.

He called up, towards the dim shape on Khush's back. 'Where are we going?'

Even through the fog, he could see how impatiently Cissie turned. 'Where? Up river, of course. The river must come from the mountains. If we follow it, we'll be able to get back over them.'

'But it'll soon be light.'

'Then we'll find a barn to hide in.'

A barn? Tad knew plenty of barns, but he'd never known one where an elephant could hide unnoticed. And were they going to *walk* back over the mountains?

'Well?' Cissie snapped. 'Have you got a better plan?'

'I—' Tad stuttered and fell silent. How could he make a plan? He couldn't even walk across a room without doing something wrong. It was better to keep quiet and obey orders.

But Cissie had snapped louder than she meant to. Away to their left, a light flickered and a few seconds later a voice called out.

'Hey? *Wer ist das?*'

Cissie threw her shawl over the lantern and she and Tad froze. Khush turned towards the voice and flapped his ears, but he didn't make a sound.

The man called again. 'I woke three times tonight already. It is enough. Your noise was joking?'

He sounded irritable and determined. Slowly, the light of the lantern grew closer.

'What for a joke is that, that wakes an old man?'

43

Tad's mind raced, but there was nothing he could do. Their best chance was to keep very still and hope the old man missed them in the fog. Any movement was sure to give them away.

The lantern stopped, moved sideways and came towards them from another angle. And, suddenly, he was there. A tall, gaunt old man, peering out of the fog not ten feet away from them. His hair hung long and grey on either side of his face and his dirty, worn shirt flapped out over his trousers.

Lantern held high, he stared at Khush with wide, disbelieving eyes.

'*Lieber Gott!*' he breathed. '*Lieber Gott in Himmel!*'

CHAPTER 8

CISSIE REACTED while Tad was still catching his breath.

'Please!' she said. 'Oh, *please*!'

She swung her leg over Khush's neck and slithered eight feet to the ground, falling into the pool of lantern light in front of Tad. The old man held out a hand to pull her up, and she grabbed it with both hers.

'Please hide us! I don't know who you are, but you have a kind face! We're being followed by enemies who want to steal my elephant and there's no one else to help us!'

By the end of the speech she was on her knees, looking pleadingly up at him. The fog swirled round her and the yellow light fell bright on her tumbled hair and her small, desperate face.

The old man looked bewildered. 'I'm thirty years here— and I never saw a child with an elephant.'

'He *is* my elephant!' Cissie said earnestly. 'He's all I have, in the whole, wide world.'

'It's the truth,' said Tad.

'There is a boy also?' The old man peered forward into the fog. 'Come here, boy!'

Nervously, Tad walked into the light.

'Closer!'

The old man shook his hand free of Cissie's and beckoned impatiently. When Tad was within reach, he grabbed his chin and jerked it round, so that Tad was forced to stare straight into his eyes.

'What is it that she tells me? There are enemies?'

'Not enemies exactly—' Tad began to gabble. 'A man says he bought the elephant from Cissie's father—just before the crash—but the money was an insult—and the writing on the paper was the wrong colour—and—'

45

His stuttered words dissolved, ridiculously, into silence and he wondered why he had spoken at all.

The old man's watery grey eyes scanned his face. 'I see that it will take much telling. Perhaps you shall take the elephant into my barn. Then we may talk.'

'Oh, thank you! Thank you!' Cissie jumped up and clasped her hands under her chin. 'I *knew* you had a kind face. Come on, Tad. We're safe!'

Safe? Tad thought of dogs, and hesitated.

'It is not well?' the old man said. He was watching Tad very closely. 'You do not trust me?'

'Of course I do. But—'

'But nothing!' Cissie said impatiently, scowling at him. 'Don't waste time, Tad. They'll be after us as soon as it's light.'

The old man held up his hand. 'First we will hear the boy. What troubles you?'

'W-well,' Tad stammered. It felt wrong to argue with Cissie, but he had to say it. 'If they follow us, they may bring dogs. And the scent will stop here. And—'

The old man gave a long, slow nod. 'That is careful. I like a careful boy. Take the elephant on, upwards of the river, and then return. We shall wait here.'

Cissie pushed her lantern into Tad's hands. 'Go on, then. I'll stay and explain everything.'

Tad hadn't expected to be sent on his own, but he didn't dare to argue any more. He lifted the lantern high, trying to see Khush's head.

'Move up. Let's get going.'

His voice sounded feeble and uncertain, drifting uselessly into the fog. Khush turned towards Cissie and flapped his ears.

'Move up!' Tad said, more firmly.

One huge front foot rose into the air. Slowly, tugging at the water plants as he went, Khush ambled on up the river.

Before they had gone twenty yards, the old man's lantern was invisible. For a few steps more, Tad could hear the rise and fall of Cissie's voice as she began her explanation and then that, too, disappeared. There was nothing but the rush of the river and the shadowy bulk of Khush as he moved steadily along the bank, his feet squelching in the wet mud.

Once or twice, lights glimmered, far to the right or left. Twice, river creatures scuttled out of the undergrowth and dived into the water. For half a mile or more, Tad peered into the fog and strained his ears to catch every sound.

It was an empty world, where the two of them walked alone, wrapped up together. When Tad gave the order to stop, he said it without thinking, as he might have spoken to a person.

'Steady. Stop now, Khush.'

The words sounded piping and thin, but Khush stopped straight away and Tad smiled.

'Now we're going to fool Mr Jackson.'

For a second he wondered what he was doing, talking to a dumb creature. But out there, in the fog, it seemed the natural thing to do. Khush bent his head and his little eyes gleamed in the lantern light.

'We're going to walk back with our feet in the water, so that we don't leave footprints. So get over now.'

Khush's trunk tickled him behind the ear.

'Stop playing around. Get over!'

The trunk tickled him behind the other ear, and he almost wished that he had the bullhook. He didn't know what would happen if he lost control.

'Khush!'

Dipping his trunk into the river, Khush pulled it out and squirted the ground, just in front of Tad's feet.

'You—!' Tad jumped backwards.

Immediately, Khush dipped his trunk in once more, and sent a new jet of water hissing on to the ground. Just missing Tad again.

It was impossible not to jump back. And straight away more water hit the ground, on the very spot he had just left.

He was being teased.

There was no mistaking it. As he backed away, step by step, Khush squirted again, with a perfect aim. Never hitting Tad's feet, but always close enough to make him jump away.

47

When Tad had been teased in school, it was always meant unkindly. And Aunt Adah had never had time for anything except work. This game was gentle and amiable, and for a moment he was completely bewildered by it.

Then, suddenly, he imagined how the two of them must look. A boy and an elephant, standing alone in the fog and playing with water. Forgetting all about where he was, and who might be listening, he started to laugh.

As though that was what he had been waiting for, Khush veered right, and splashed down into the river. It was much deeper than Tad had expected. A wave lapped over the bank and for a second Khush disappeared completely under the dark water, medicine boxes and all. Then he surfaced, like a small island, with water streaming from his body.

'This way. Come here, Khush.'

Walking backwards down the bank, Tad called softly and Khush began to plod steadily after him, parting the water like a barge, while Tad held the lantern high to keep him in sight.

It seemed a long time before they saw the answering lantern, and heard Cissie call.

'Is that you, Tad? Come to the ramp.'

There was a curious, cobbled ramp leading up out of the river. It looked like some kind of slipway. Tad couldn't quite make out what it was for, but he was glad there was somewhere that Khush could climb out without marking the bank.

'I've explained *everything*,' Cissie said eagerly. 'And Mr Nagel says Khush can hide in his barn until tomorrow night.'

Tad looked over her shoulder, at the old man. 'Thank you very much.' He had not realized, until then, how cold and tired he was. 'Get over! Up on the bank, Khush!'

'Come here, Khush!' Cissie said. 'Come to the barn.'

Khush heaved himself out of the water, huge and dripping, and marched up the ramp, his chain scraping on the cobbles. Tad pulled a stray branch from the flood debris caught in the reeds and brushed away any stray elephant prints as he followed.

'A good, careful boy,' said a voice behind him. Mr Nagel

was watching, with the lantern held high and a strange, sad smile on his face. 'Miss Keenan is lucky for a friend.'

It seemed odd to be called Cissie's friend. Awkwardly, Tad swirled his branch again, wiping out the last print. Then he turned and stepped into the barn.

It was a large, solid building, set well back from the river. But its doors hung askew on their hinges and it smelt of neglect. Old, rotting sacks were tossed into one corner, and mouldering harness drooped on hooks, above a stack of withered roots.

The most curious thing of all hung from the roof. It was a long wooden platform, with a high raised edge, and it was suspended by ropes tied to its four corners. Tad took a few steps nearer, frowning up at it, and he heard Mr Nagel chuckle drily.

'You do not know what is that? Ha?'

'Is it some kind of grain store?'

'I use him for a grain store now. See the rings, to stop rats climbing down the ropes? But in the beginning—no, it was not for that.' Mr Nagel's face twisted.

'Looks like a giant box,' Cissie said flippantly. 'Have you got a lid for it?'

Mr Nagel looked at her for a moment. Then at Tad. Then he marched down the barn and began to unwind one of the ropes. 'I will show you.'

There was a peculiar grimness in his voice and Cissie moved closer to Tad. 'Do you think he's—all right?'

Tad looked down the barn. One corner of the platform was hanging free now, and Mr Nagel was panting slightly as he struggled with a second rope.

'Don't think he'll do us any harm,' he whispered back. 'And we've got nowhere else to go.'

Grunting as he took the strain, the old man let out the second rope. One end of the wooden platform swung loose and rattled down to the ground, hitting it with a thump. Khush raised his trunk and snorted loudly, stamping his feet on the floor of the barn.

'Well, boy?' said Mr Nagel, gasping from the effort. He

stepped back and gave Tad a challenging look. 'What for a grain store is *that*?'

Tad walked slowly down the barn until he was standing at the lowered end of the platform. As Cissie had said, it was like a box. A shallow wooden box, around twenty feet long by ten feet wide. In the centre was a roughly-built clapboard hut, with a single window and a pitched roof.

'Looks like—' He hesitated. What he was thinking seemed too strange to be true.

'I can see in your head,' Mr Nagel said sadly. 'You think like all my neighbours, that I am an old crazy. The man with a boat in his barn, instead of good cows.'

Tad shuffled uneasily. The old man's pale eyes were fixed on his face, waiting for something.

'Why shouldn't you have a boat?' Cissie said briskly. 'You're here by the river. You might as well row out on it from time to time. Don't you think so, Tad?'

Tad looked at the wooden box. He'd seen flatboats like that on the Tamaquon, and he knew what they were for. Not the kind of rowing picnic that Cissie had in mind. They could only travel down river, with the current. On one-way journeys.

Mr Nagel was still watching him. Tad stuttered out the question in his mind.

'Are—are you fixing to go west? Is that why you built it?'

'West?' The old man said the word bitterly, as if it were a lemon in his mouth. 'What is *west* for a man with no sons? When I had two boys like you, *then* I was fixing to go west. With Franz and Heinrich—and Greta.' He gasped a little, catching his breath.

'I'm sorry,' Tad said. 'Did they—?'

Cissie scowled, warning him to stop. Mr Nagel's face had gone stark white, with the beard stubble standing out dark and ragged. But he went on talking as soon as he could speak.

'They told me—after the cholera—that I should take a new wife. Make new sons. As if—as if a man could forget, and wipe away what has been.'

Cissie sidled close to Tad again, and he saw her eyes widen

nervously, but Mr Nagel didn't notice. Whatever he saw, it was not the two of them. It was not even Khush, tweaking shrivelled turnips from a sack. He tugged at his ragged grey hair and looked at the flatboat.

'A man with two boys has a reason. He can build such a boat. He can take all he owns—cows and chickens and pigs— and set off light in the heart. But a widow man? A childless man?'

He looked at Tad hungrily, searching for something that wasn't there.

'I'm sorry—' Tad said.

Mr Nagel shook his head. 'I told you already—I am an old crazy. But I like to tell my tale. And to show my poor little craft, who will never go down the river now.'

He picked up one of the slack ropes and began to tug at it, heaving the flatboat back up towards the roof. Tad went to help him, gripping the rope and pulling in time.

As the end started to lift from the floor, Khush ambled forward to examine it, idly tossing out a few wisps of hay that he found inside.

And in that instant, as Khush stood there and Mr Nagel and Tad hauled on the rope, Cissie yelled.

'No! Don't pull it up!'

'What?' Tad turned to stare at her. 'What's the matter, Cissie?'

She didn't answer. Instead, she came forward and grabbed the old man's sleeve. 'Did you say that people take animals in boats like that? Cows? And horses?'

Mr Nagel blinked at her, bewildered by her fierceness. 'Of course. I have seen it many times.'

'Then it's not a poor little craft!' Cissie said triumphantly. She laid a hand on the flatboat's wooden side. 'It *can* go west. Give it to us, and we'll take it!'

'West?' Tad's head spun. 'But we're going east, Miss Cissie. Over the mountains.'

'Not any more!' Cissie was bubbling with excitement. She ran her hands lovingly over the flatboat. 'Don't you see? We can put Khush in here and disappear down the river.'

51

'You mean—' The whole thing sounded impossible. Tad couldn't believe she meant it.

But she did. She gripped his shoulder and spun him round, so that he could see Khush and the boat together. And her voice was fierce and determined.

'We're going to Nebraska!'

Oh, Ketty!

Remember how Pa used to say *God means us to do it*! When he got a notion, and his eyes lit up and there was no shifting him. Remember?

Now I know how he felt.

God means us to come straight to you.

It could not be plainer. Yesterday, I rescued Khush from the thieves who had taken him, and set off on my own, with the elephant boy Pa hired in Ginder Falls. My only idea was to head back east. To find some decent lodging in Philadelphia and wait for you to tell me I could come.

But God has found me a boat. One that can carry Khush! And, as if that were not miracle enough, it is a boat that can travel *only west*!

I shall come to you down the Ohio river, carried on the April flood. Tad (the boy Pa hired) will help me and protect me. He does not seem to have much in the way of brains, but he is biddable and very large and strong.

We set sail this evening, as soon as it is dark. I think it is no use, now, to post this long letter, because we shall be with you SO SOON!! I shall continue the tale of our adventures, so that you can share them, but I shall be my own postman!

CHAPTER 9

'BUT THE Ohio doesn't *go* to Nebraska,' Tad said. 'You heard Mr Nagel. His boat can only take you as far as Cairo. In Illinois. After that, you'd have to go *up* the Mississippi and then *up* the Missouri. And flatboats can't go upstream.'

'Don't argue!' Cissie snapped. 'We're going.'

Tad sighed and went on filing through Khush's chain. They had been arguing for an hour, and Cissie was white with exhaustion, but he couldn't get her to change her mind. She stood straight and stubborn, glaring at him as she gave her orders.

Crazy orders.

Tad had tried saying that he wouldn't come, but Cissie wouldn't take any notice.

'You *must* come. Mr Nagel won't give us the boat unless you do. *You're* the one who reminds him of his sons.'

'And if I say no—'

'I'll go anyway! Whether you come or not! And if I get scalped, on the other side of the Mississippi, it will be all your fault.'

'But if you can't have the boat—'

'I'll get it! If Mr Nagel won't give it to me, Khush and I will drag it out on our own. In the dark. I'm going to Nebraska! And Khush is coming with me!'

Khush looked up from the turnips he was eating and gazed mildly at the two of them.

'The Ohio doesn't *go* to Nebraska,' Tad said.

'You see? I'll get lost if you don't come.'

It was impossible to discuss it properly. The idea was burning her up. She talked as though they would glide down the Ohio—a thousand miles from Pittsburgh to Cairo—in two or three sunny days. And then, somehow, *up* the

Mississippi and the Missouri. With Khush standing stock still all the way.

On a *river*.

Tad knew about rivers. He had been in little boats with Aunt Adah's lodgers. He had fallen in the Tamaquon five times and nearly drowned twice. Cissie's plan was ridiculous.

But no one listened to him. Cissie ignored what he said and Mr Nagel didn't even hear. He was too busy walking backwards and forwards between the house and the barn, heaping up things they might need, next to the boxes of medicine bottles.

Old grey blankets. A bag of dried apple rings. Sharp knives and tin mugs and half a sack of flour.

His cheeks were a hectic red and his eyes glowed obsessively. 'I have a map for you. Also a bucket, and a sickle to cut food for the elephant, because you must feed him from the banks of the river. A spade also. With such a creature, eating so much, it will be hard to keep the boat clean—'

Tad couldn't help getting involved. All his life he had been doing what he was told and he didn't know how to go on resisting. Anyway, Cissie and Mr Nagel had answers for everything.

'There's no reason to worry about *money*! We've got Khush. We can make money whenever we choose—'

'—and you come at the right time!' Mr Nagel interrupted jubilantly. 'The river floods. It covers the rocks already, all the way down—'

'But—'

Even Khush had caught the excitement in the air. He kept sidling up to Mr Nagel's heap, tweaking the blankets and sneaking his trunk into the dried apples. Tad couldn't stand out against them all.

And then Mr Jackson came.

Towards the end of the morning, when the heap in the barn was as tall as Cissie, Mr Nagel burst in empty-handed.

'There are riders! And dogs! Keep the elephant still, and I will make a fire to hide his scent.'

He tugged at the rotting sacks in the corner, staggering out with one huge armful and coming back for another. There was already a stack of boxes and old magazines on the sloping ground between the barn and the river and he flung the old sacks on top of the pile.

Going to swing the barn door shut, Tad saw him sprinkle the heap with kerosene. He threw in a match and the whole lot went up with a scorching crackle, followed by a steady column of foul, sluggish smoke.

Khush snorted uneasily as the smell drifted into the barn.

'Steady there, Khush! Steady!'

Tad ran towards him, crooning in his throat, and Cissie stroked his neck and muttered.

'Easy, Khush! Quiet now!'

He was already excited and he began to shuffle his feet, heading for the door. Cissie grabbed up the bullhook and waved it in front of him.

'Lie down, Khush! Lie *down*!'

Khush made a sound like a sigh and lumbered down on to his knees. Then he lurched over sideways and stretched out on the floor of the barn.

'Good boy. *Good* boy.' Cissie crouched beside his head, and pointed at the barn door. 'Go and take a look, Tad.'

Tad crept to the side, where the door hung away from its hinges, and peered through the gap. Smoke still hung in the air, but the fire was dying down and he could see people talking to Mr Nagel.

There were half a dozen of them. Esther sat high on a horse, her purple feathers bobbing, but Mr Jackson and the men from the livery stables had dismounted. One of them held two yelping dogs that strained at their collars, shying away from the fire and sniffing the ground beside the river.

Tad could just make out what Mr Nagel was saying, above the yelps.

'I saw no elephant. No giraffe, no *Nilpferd*, no wild animals. I sleep fast, and I have no dog.'

56

Mr Jackson was staring hard at him. 'We know the animal came this way.'

Mr Nagel shrugged. 'I saw no elephant.'

'We have to find it!' Esther leaned down towards him and, even through the smoke, Tad saw the false sweetness of her smile. 'You will help us, won't you, Mr Nagel? Those children mustn't get away with it.'

The fumes from the fire caught the back of her throat, and she began to cough, bent forward over her horse's neck. Mr Jackson ran a finger absently over her ankle.

'The dogs want to go on. We'll let them follow the scent and maybe we'll catch up with them in an hour or so. But if not—'

He swivelled back to face Mr Nagel and there was nothing absent about the way he looked at him. Even from inside the barn, Tad could feel the cold threat in his voice.

'I hope you'll send me word if you see a boy and a girl with an elephant. I bought that animal, fair and square, and I'm going to get it back. Even if I have to hunt those children from here to Philadelphia. The law is on my side, and anyone who crosses me will find that out.'

Esther patted her mouth with a lacy handkerchief. 'Don't fret, Hannibal. They won't get ten miles. How can they hide an elephant, when we've got everyone looking for them? Mr Nagel will tell us if they come by here again. *Won't* you, Mr Nagel?'

She straightened her bonnet and simpered down at him. Then she moved on up river, following the dogs. When Mr Nagel came back into the barn, he was shaking.

'To speak to me like that! And the woman! She looks at me with her painted eyes and thinks I will be the old fool for her! With her husband watching!'

Cissie stepped back, to let Khush scramble up from the floor. 'I don't believe he *is* her husband.'

Mr Nagel's mouth twisted. 'That such a woman should live! When my Greta—'

He snatched a pair of scissors from the heap he had made and looked at them savagely. Then he glared at Cissie.

57

'Come here!'

'What—?'

'Come *here!*' He waved the scissors imperiously. 'That bad woman looks for a boy and a girl and an elephant? Well, the elephant shall be hidden. And you shall be two boys who go down the river.'

Cissie hesitated for a second and then walked briskly up to him. 'All right. Go ahead!'

He grabbed a handful of her ringlets and cut into the long, bright hair.

'You can't—' Tad said.

'Of course he can! Don't be stupid!'

But Khush agreed with Tad. He flapped his ears and strode down the barn. With a sharp flourish of his trunk, he tweaked the scissors out of Mr Nagel's hand and flung them against the wall.

Cissie stamped her foot. 'Can't you keep him quiet, Tad? He thinks Mr Nagel's attacking me. Talk to him!'

'But—'

'Go *on!*'

Tad began to mutter, awkwardly. 'Steady, Khush. He's not an enemy. He's cutting Cissie's hair so that we can go to Nebraska. To—to—'

'To see Ketty!' Cissie snapped, snatching up the scissors. 'Tell him that. He likes Ketty.'

Obediently, Tad murmured the words. 'We're going to see Ketty. You know her, Khush. Going to see Ketty, in Nebraska . . . '

It seemed to work. Gradually Khush lowered his trunk and ambled back to the pile of turnips. Cissie handed the scissors to Mr Nagel and he went on cutting.

One by one, the pretty ringlets fell on to the dirty straw. Without them, Cissie's face looked bonier. Naked. When the last ringlet had fallen, Mr Nagel stepped back to take a look and she squared up to him, legs apart and head flung back.

'Do I look right?' Her hands fumbled at her waist. 'Once I've got these off, maybe—'

Skirt and petticoats rustled to the ground and, before Tad

realized what she was doing, she was standing there in her frilly white drawers with their shocking scarlet ribbons. She grinned up at him and began to stride up and down, shamelessly.

'Am I good? Will people really take me for a boy?'

Tad turned away in embarrassment, but Mr Nagel smiled.

'You are very good. I will give you Franz's clothes to wear. And both my boys will go west together.'

CHAPTER 10

THEY SPENT the rest of the day working on the flatboat. Now that Mr Nagel was angry, his head was full of plans.

'This cabin—I made it for my family. For four people. But it is too small for even one elephant. We must take away and make a cover, as for a wagon.' He pushed a handful of tools at Tad. 'You break the cabin. I will cut the trees.'

Snatching up an axe, he went, leaving Tad staring at the clapboard sides of the cabin.

'Go on!' Cissie said impatiently. 'Why are you standing there? We haven't got any time to waste.'

She grabbed a hammer and hit out wildly at the wooden walls of the cabin, sending splinters flying. Tad shook his head.

'I think I'd better—'

'Go on, then!'

She stood over him, with her hands on her hips, watching relentlessly. It was the sort of job that suited Tad, but he worked too slowly and methodically for her. She kept hovering, ready for any chance to grab the end of a plank and heave at it.

Tad tried to stop her. 'It's not suitable for you—'

'Oh, don't be so stupid!' Cissie tugged again, drove a splinter into her hand and glared at Tad as she pulled it out. 'We've all got to help, if it's going to get done.'

She spoke sulkily, but Tad could see the sense in what she said. He showed her how to lever up the long nails and knock out the wooden pegs. When Mr Nagel came back, the two of them were working hard, one on each side of the boat.

'Like two good brothers who help each other.' Mr Nagel beamed. 'Now you shall see how I make an elephant shelter. Come to bring the trees. There is no one near.'

He had cut four tall, supple saplings and trimmed off all the branches. They dragged the saplings into the barn and bent them over the top of the flatboat, fastening one end on each side, so that four long ribs curved over the middle section of the boat.

Cissie was delighted. 'There'll be plenty of room for Khush under that. All we need is something to cover it over.'

'I have tarpaulins. Three or four. And many, many blankets. The blankets will hang down, back and front, to hide the elephant.'

Mr Nagel nodded proudly at the shelter, but Tad wasn't so sure about it. He wondered how long Khush would stand still, in such a small space. But he hauled tarpaulins and draped blankets, without saying a word.

It was almost midnight before the whole thing was ready. They hitched Khush to the front of the boat and Mr Nagel flung open the big barn doors.

There was no friendly fog this time. Only low cloud and a heavy drizzle. But no one came by to disturb them as they flung sacks over the cobbled slipway.

Mr Nagel looked at Tad. 'I had two sons, one wife and a horse to pull. You think that your elephant can do it on his own?'

'Of course he can!' Cissie said, not giving Tad a chance to answer. 'Move up, Khush! It's time to go.'

Khush gave her a long, puzzled look. Then he leaned into the rope harness they had tied round him and began to heave. The boat creaked and shuddered from side to side. With a slithering scrape, it began to move slowly over the floor of the barn and out on to the ramp.

Once it was on the sloping river bank, it needed no pulling. It ran forward, against Khush's back legs, so that he was bearing its weight.

'Steady!' Cissie snapped. She waved the bullhook in his face. 'Move up slowly, now!'

Step by step, Khush moved forward, with the boat behind him, until it came to rest at the very end of the ramp, half aground and half floating.

'It is ready to load,' Mr Nagel said.

They brought the stores down and stacked them under tarpaulins, in the back and front of the boat, while Khush stood watching. Food and straw. Blankets and matches. Knives and a bucket. A small bundle of tools, wrapped in a bit of sacking.

Cissie rolled up the sleeves of Franz Nagel's shirt and turned up the trouser legs, to wade barefoot. 'Hurry! We must start while it's still night!'

Tad had once been on the Tamaquon at night, and it had frightened him to death, but he didn't say so. He did as he was told, loading stores and carrying down the long, heavy sweep-oar that went at the back, to steer the boat.

At the end, when everything else was on, Cissie took Khush up to the barn again and brought him down with the boxes of medicine bottles. Tad stared.

'We're not taking *those*?'

'Of course we are.' Cissie tossed her head. 'You don't think I'm leaving them behind, for Mr Jackson to find?'

Tad nudged her and glanced towards Mr Nagel. All he meant was that she was being tactless, but she misunderstood him. She turned to the old man and grinned.

'There's no way I can pay you for what you've given us. Unless you'd like some of this tincture. The recipe comes from India—'

'And it cures all sickness?' Mr Nagel looked amused. 'I have heard of such medicines. Let me see.'

Cissie pulled out a bottle and held it up to him. In the lantern light, the green liquid swirled mistily, full of strange lights and shadows.

Mr Nagel held the bottle carefully and looked down at it. 'I shall not drink the medicine. But I shall keep it. And when I see the green—then I will think of you, going west in my boat. Maybe, after all, it will cure what ails me.' He held out his hand. 'We must say goodbye, before you go on board.'

Tad took the hand and shook it. The grasp was firm, but Mr Nagel's skin was slack and liver-spotted. He was a very old man and his eyes wavered as he looked into Tad's face.

'You will take care? And come to the West?'

'Of course we will!' said Cissie. 'Goodbye. And thank you.'

'Thank you very much,' Tad said softly.

Mr Nagel was still holding his hand. Now he opened his fingers slowly and let it go. 'You must put your elephant on board.'

'That's right.' Cissie waved her hand towards the flatboat. 'Come on, Khush. Move up!'

Khush lifted his head warily.

'Oh come on! Don't be a baby. This end of the boat is on dry land. Move up!'

She grabbed the bullhook out of the boat and Khush looked at it, his eyes travelling along the short, straight handle to the curved metal prong at the end. Very slowly and deliberately, he took a step backwards, away from the boat.

Cissie glared and moved towards him with the bullhook.

'Not like that,' Tad muttered. It was mad to start out with an angry, sulky elephant. They would all be drowned. Jumping into the boat, he held out his hands. 'Come here, Khush! Come here!'

Khush released his breath in a gigantic sigh that shook his whole body. He took one step forward and then stopped and glanced at Cissie.

'Get on board, Miss Cissie,' Tad said. 'He needs to know you're going too. Get on!'

He didn't look at her, because he was too busy watching Khush, but he heard her gasp. Then she scrambled into the boat.

Mr Nagel chuckled, hardly loud enough to hear. 'So, just so, it was with Franz and Heinrich . . . '

Tad crooned the order again, quite softly. 'Come here, Khush.'

Khush lifted his great feet, one after another, and stepped into the boat, moving so delicately that he did not even brush the wooden sides.

Immediately, Cissie took charge. 'Get the oar, Tad. I'll move him down the boat, to lift it off the bottom.'

Tad picked up the long oar, reversing it so that the pole was ready to push as she led Khush away from the bank. The flatboat dipped, its landward end scraping through the mud with a loud sucking noise, and Tad leaned against the pole, pushing hard.

For a few seconds, they were neither afloat nor aground. Then the back end of the boat swung round, so that the whole thing was moving away from the bank. They were on the river. With an elephant on board. Tad gave one last push, shoving the boat out into deep water.

Lantern held high, Mr Nagel stood on the bank in a tiny patch of light, not waving but staring after them. The boat he had built twenty years before began to move steadily away, heading west at last.

Tad turned the sweep the right way round and tried to steer, but it was impossible to do much. He could only concentrate on staying in clear water, well away from the banks. Cissie crouched beside Khush, tying his tethering ropes and hobbling his legs in a figure of eight.

In a few minutes, the shadowy buildings of Pittsburgh began to rise around them, their black shapes shutting out the stars. Here and there a fire glowed, or voices sounded from the shore, but the river round the boat was dark and empty.

Drifting up to the Point, where the Allegheny and Monongahela rivers met, they hit a patch of turbulence. For a while, Tad was too busy to think about anything except the balance of the boat and the way the water slapped against its sides. The sweep was hard to handle and once or twice they lurched frighteningly.

Then they were clear of the Point, and out into the main river at last. The water steadied and the Ohio current took them.

We have done it! We are here, on the river, *speeding*
down towards the Mississippi. Khush must be the only
elephant ever to sail these waters, but you would never
guess it, from the calm way he stands under his canopy,
chewing.

I knew that I was right, from the very beginning, but I
had to fight for *hours* to get Tad to agree. I fear he has a
cowardly heart, for he produced a mountain of small
objections, setting up a new one each time I demolished
the one before. He had not the spirit to grasp the
beautiful simplicity of my plan. But I knew that if I
insisted enough he would *obey orders*, as Pa paid him to.
And so it proved.

He may be harder to manage from now on, though,
for I have taken on a new identity. My petticoats and
ringlets have disappeared! I am Franz Nagel, younger son
of the good angel who provided our boat. In the perilous
circumstances in which we find ourselves, it will be a
good disguise, but it will make it harder for me to keep
Tad in his place. For a moment, as we boarded the boat,
he attempted to give orders to *me*!

But I shall not waver. Whatever I have done, I know
that this is right. And maybe it will make up for other
things.

CHAPTER 11

TAD LEANED against the long stern oar, trying to hold the flatboat to a straight course. He wished they had never set out.

Khush had been restless from the very beginning. Now it was light, he had started rubbing his shoulders against the sides of his shelter and trampling the dirty straw into a stinking mess.

The river was getting busy, with boats travelling downstream from Pittsburgh, and people looked curiously at the bobbing flatboat. Men leaned out of towboats and steamboats and little stern-wheelers to shout at Tad.

He mumbled apologies and tried to steer closer to the bank, but it was hard to stay out of trouble. A huge coal tow overtook them, the steamer at the back of it pushing fifteen long, low barges. Its wake set them juddering wildly and water slopped over the sides of the boat.

Inside the shelter, Khush rumbled and rocked.

'Can't you keep him still?' Tad said. He didn't even notice how sharp he sounded, but Cissie glared as she put away the paper she was writing on.

She began to croon at Khush, in a high, sing-song voice. 'Steady, there. Don't move. We're going to see Ketty, in Nebraska. She'll make us apple pie and cornbread and let me brush her beautiful hair . . . '

Khush snorted inside the shelter, but he stopped moving so wildly.

'She'll sit in the garden and sing,' Cissie crooned. 'Everything will be all right when we get to her house . . . '

Tad leaned on the oar and let a picture take shape inside his head. A white frame house, with a porch and big windows. Light and airy. Smelling wonderfully of baking.

' . . . remember, Khush,' Cissie was murmuring now, 'how

all her clothes are trimmed with lace. And her shoes are too small for anyone else but me to wear. When she brushes her hair at night, the sparks crackle . . . '

Tad half-closed his eyes, imagining a figure with tiny feet and long, floating hair. A woman who stood by the white house, in a cool, green garden.

And Khush settled down and dipped his trunk into the bucket, sucking noisily.

Cissie managed to keep him calm—more or less—until the end of the day. By then, all his food and drink had gone, and the narrow shelter was filthy. In the twilight, they beached the boat by a quiet creek and Tad started to fork out the dirty straw, so that he could scrub the boards.

For ten minutes, Cissie stood and watched. For the first time, Tad wondered how it was that she gave all the orders and he did all the work. He forked, and scraped the boards fiercely, and forked again.

'You look as though you could use some help,' Cissie said.

Grinning with surprise, Tad spun round.

'If you're offering—'

'Me?'

'I thought you meant—' His grin vanished and he went red.

'I meant Khush, of course. I could teach him a new command. Come on, Khush! Clear ship!'

Khush was off among the trees, twenty yards away, but Cissie ordered him back. She began to teach him to pick up the straw Tad raked, waving the bullhook at him when he tried to wander off. After a while, he got the hang of it, and the work speeded up.

But even with Khush's help, it took several hours to clean out the boat. And when that was done, they still had to cut enough greenery to feed him all the next day.

Tad knew he couldn't do it. Not on his own. He leaned on the pitchfork and looked at Cissie.

'There's going to be days of this,' he said carefully. 'And I need to sleep sometimes.'

Cissie gave him a long, wary stare. Then she patted Khush's shoulder. 'Go play, Khush.'

The elephant ambled away to eat, and Cissie picked the

sickle out of the bottom of the boat. 'I'll cut the fodder, and you can carry it.'

It was an order, not a question, but Tad was too tired to resent the way she said it. He followed her into the trees, ready to scoop up what she cut.

They managed a couple of hours sleep before dawn. Then they persuaded Khush back into the boat by pretending to leave without him. Cissie untied the ropes and Tad picked up the oar and began to push the boat free of the mud. Khush charged towards them, stepping on board so fast that he almost turned the boat over.

But he was awkward. He let Cissie tie his tethers, but when she picked up the rope to hobble his legs, he stepped sideways and rattled his trunk angrily against the boards.

Cissie gave up. She twitched down the blankets to hide him, muttering furiously.

'Ketty would be disgusted! She was always so pleased to see you well-trained . . . '

But that had no effect on Khush. He was much more restless than the day before, rocking the boat hard and making loud, badtempered noises. Tad struggled to keep them in the channel, worrying all the time that they would capsize, and Cissie chanted desperately about Ketty. But it was no use.

As they floated down towards Wheeling, Khush snatched at the blankets with his trunk and tugged them away from in front of him. Trumpeting triumphantly, he dropped them and reached for the saplings that arched above his head.

'No, Khush! No!' yelled Cissie.

Khush ignored her. He wrenched the saplings away from the sides of the boat and threw them disdainfully into the river, leaving himself completely exposed.

It was the worst possible moment. They were just drifting into the bustle of boats round Wheeling, and people began to shout straight away.

'There's an elephant!'

'Well, dang my—'

'Take a look at that!'

Towboats and rowing boats, skiffs and canoes came

scurrying out to take a closer look. Men on the quay waved their hats or scratched their heads, and children pointed and yelled.

'Where'd you get it?'

'Ain't you got no ma or pa with you?'

'Are you with a circus?'

Khush was delighted. He waved his trunk and trumpeted and tossed straw into the air. The crowd laughed, and he responded by squirting water at the boats and catching at the pieces of bread that people threw.

It was the passengers on the up-river steamboat who began to throw money. A drunken man on a high deck tossed a dollar, and Khush caught it neatly in his trunk.

There was an enormous cheer. Nickels and dimes—even a few more dollars—rained down into the boat for ten or fifteen minutes. Each time Khush caught something, there was a roar of appreciation, followed by more money.

Cissie smiled and waved, but Tad kept his head down and went on steering. He wanted to get away from the crowds, but it wasn't easy. People from Wheeling followed them down river, and boats coming up turned round and floated back the way they had come.

When the crush finally thinned, Cissie fell to her knees to pick up the money.

'Look, Tad! Twenty dollars and seventeen cents! And three buttons and a British penny. *Look* at it all. If this happens at every town, we can take the railroad once we're over the Mississippi. *And* hire a special car for Khush.'

Tad didn't answer, and she looked up at him.

'What's the matter? Why are you staring at me like that?'

'I—like what?' He had been wishing that Khush was safely hidden away. Had it shown in his face?

Cissie flung the money on to the boards and glared at him. 'You're looking at me as if I'd done something wrong! As if I were—It's not your business to have opinions about me!'

'I haven't! I didn't do anything!'

Tad was bewildered. He couldn't imagine what had upset her, but something certainly had.

'Keep your eyes to yourself!' She turned away and began to pick up the money all over again.

Tad bit back the things he would have liked to say. But, silently, he was worrying about them.

All the people on the steamboat would be in Pittsburgh soon. And Pittsburgh would be humming with stories about an elephant on a boat. It wouldn't be long before Mr Jackson heard.

It took longer than Tad expected. For another three days, they travelled down the Ohio, stopping off at night to clean the boat and collect fodder. The boat was beginning to get very unpleasant, because there was no shelter from the rain. They had to stack everything high, to keep it out of the muck that swirled round their ankles.

But Cissie wouldn't hear of abandoning the boat. She turned savage when Tad suggested that they might travel by land.

'What do you know about it? We have to stay on the river —or it'll take *months* to get to Ketty.'

So on they went. And every day there were more boats, and more curious people staring at Khush.

On the third day, as the sun began to set, they came past Parkersburg, sweeping under the bridge in midstream. The sky was a glorious gold, but the water was black, lapping coldly round the flatboat. Tad hoped they might slip past unnoticed, but obviously someone had been watching out for Khush. A little flock of boats put out from the town the moment he was sighted and Cissie smiled and waved, hoping for more money.

But this time it was different. As the boats came towards them, someone called from the little steamboat at the front.

'Ship your oar! We're going to put a line aboard and tow you in to the bank!'

It was a stocky, red-faced man in a smart coat and a tall hat. He did not expect to be disobeyed.

Cissie clambered on to the medicine boxes, so that he could see her properly. 'We don't want to come ashore. Thank you.'

The red-faced man spluttered and there were chuckles from

the boat behind. Cissie grinned, taking the chuckles for applause, but Tad did not smile.

The man raised his voice. 'We have received a telegraph message asking us to stop a boy and a girl passing down the river with an elephant. We believe that the elephant was stolen.'

'He was not!' Cissie shouted. 'He belongs to me!'

But the man did not pay any attention. Another man, small and bespectacled, was pulling at his sleeve.

'Mr Worthington. We should consider—'

He whispered busily, and the red-faced man sighed.

'For heaven's sake, Crisman, what does it matter that there's no girl? Do you think there's another elephant afloat on this river? This is certainly the stolen animal. The owner is on his way with the documents.'

'Fake papers!' Cissie said passionately. 'Forged!'

Mr Worthington frowned. 'That can be settled legally, once we're ashore.'

Tad didn't like the word *legally*. Mr Jackson's receipt had looked legal. Much more legal than anything he and Cissie had. He leaned over and hissed in her ear.

'We mustn't land!'

'If you won't come sensibly,' bellowed Mr Worthington, 'I shall get someone to board you!'

Cissie looked scornful. 'Just let them try!'

One of the boatmen threw a rope, and she knocked it into the water. Then she bent down to untie Khush's tethers.

'Come on, Khush!' she shouted. 'Clear ship!' Picking up a handful of the day's dirty straw, she flung it, as hard as she could, towards the steamboat.

It fell harmlessly into the water between the two boats and disappeared in the darkness. But Khush was watching with interest. Scooping up a bundle of straw, he stood staring at the steamboat, his trunk swinging.

'Clear ship!' yelled Cissie.

Khush's aim was much better than hers. He hit Mr Worthington full in the face. The face turned almost purple and Mr Worthington spat filthy straw.

71

'Get that animal!' he shouted.

'Go on, Khush,' said Cissie, joyfully. 'Clear ship!'

Stinking straw began to fly everywhere, filling the air and raining down into the surrounding boats. Desperately, Mr Worthington shouted to his crew.

'They're only a couple of children! Someone get on board!'

The men backed away.

'Children ain't no problem, sir. But that creature—'

'Man'd be crazy to tangle with an animal like that.'

'Best go yourself, if you're so keen to have it done.'

It was growing darker all the time. The sun was down now, and the boats behind began to move closer, to see what was happening. One or two people called out encouragement to Cissie and Tad.

'We can't have people laughing at the law.' Mr Worthington drew himself up pompously. 'Someone must put a tow-rope on that boat.' He looked round and saw the little, bespectacled clerk who had whispered in his ear. 'You'll have to do it, Crisman.'

'Me, Mr Worthington?'

'You, Crisman!'

Cissie snatched the sweep-oar from Tad and swung it wildly across the surface of the water. 'If anyone tries to board us, I'll knock him in the river!'

Mr Worthington took no notice. He waved his hand imperiously, ordering the steamboat closer to the raft.

'Now, Crisman!'

Tad thought he actually pushed the little clerk, but he couldn't be sure. Things happened very quickly.

Cissie swung the sweep, but she was too late. Mr Crisman landed on top of her, knocking her down into the bottom of the boat. It was an accident, but Khush roared with rage and started forward.

Tad raced too, and grabbed Mr Crisman, but that didn't stop Khush. He thought Cissie was being attacked, and he charged to help her. The flatboat tilted wildly.

Cissie grabbed the side, but Tad and Mr Crisman, still entangled with each other, were flung backwards into the

72

water, in a rain of boxes and bundles.

As Tad struggled to get free, there was another, gigantic splash and then a despairing wail from Cissie.

'Look what you've done! You've drowned my elephant!'

CHAPTER 12

THE WATER went wild. Mr Crisman struggled towards the steamboat, kicking Tad in the side of the head, and Khush thrashed furiously as he sank under the surface. The whole river was a boiling, churning chaos, with every boat rocking crazily.

The only thing to do was get away. Dizzy, with his lungs near bursting, Tad dived under the flatboat and worked his way along its bottom. He came up at the far end, twenty feet away from Cissie. She was still in the boat, baling madly with the bucket, and, when she saw Mr Crisman being hauled on to the steamboat, she shrieked at him.

'Why are they bothering with you? What about my elephant? And my—brother?'

'They'll be up in a moment,' Mr Worthington snapped. 'They must have gone right to the bottom.'

'To the *bottom*? What do you think an elephant is? Some kind of water creature? And what about Tad?'

I'm here. The words were ready on Tad's lips, and he had his hand out to grab the back of the boat. In a minute, he would have hauled himself on board, but just as he was about to speak, a movement caught his eye. Twenty or thirty yards downstream, a black hump was travelling away from him, through the dark water.

At first he thought it was one of the boxes of medicine bottles, floating away down the river. But it wasn't drifting. It surged forward in bursts, accelerating and then slowing, out of time with the steady run of the current. Tad couldn't hear anything except the shouting and splashing behind him, but he could see the power in those movements.

Slipping quietly away from the boats, into the darkness, he started to swim downsteam, after the hump. It was hard to keep in sight in the twilight, but he swam as hard as he could and gradually he gained on it.

By the time he was ten yards away, he could see clearly. Khush was in front of him, completely submerged except for his head. He was not being carried helplessly by the current. He was swimming.

It was another twenty minutes before Tad caught up. By then, they were well downstream, out of sight of Parkersburg. Tad drew level, keeping his distance from the churning water, and called softly.

'Hallo, Khush.'

Khush lifted his head and gave a small, delighted squeal. Then he turned left, towards the West Virginia bank.

'No!' Tad hissed. There wasn't enough cover there. 'No, Khush! Move up!' He was too cold and tired to make a proper plan, but he knew that they had to hide. 'Move up, Khush!'

The great head turned towards him in the dark, veering right again. For a second, Khush's skin brushed his leg. Its roughness had a familiar, reassuring feel and Tad began to swim harder, towards a clump of trees on the other shore, in Ohio.

It was a good quarter of a mile away, growing on a sandbar that stuck out into the water. Tad thought that he and Khush could reach it. He was getting cold and tired, but Khush was near enough to cling to. Fixing his eyes on the trees, he headed towards them.

A little bay had formed inside the curve of the sandbank, littered with logs and debris that had floated down and caught on the bar. Wearily, Tad dragged himself up the gritty beach, knocking his feet on every obstacle.

With a huge squelch, Khush lumbered out of the water and followed Tad on to the sandbank. It was only ten or fifteen yards wide, but the trees and bushes were thick enough to hide them. They could rest there for the night, and keep an eye on the river.

Tad knew they ought to go back to Parkersburg, to find out what had happened to Cissie. But they were on the wrong side of the river now, and he was so exhausted that he could hardly move. Even Khush dragged his feet as they struggled through the trees, and as soon as Tad told him to stop he lay down.

Tad stripped off his wet clothes, wrung them out and hung them on the bushes to dry. Then he crawled close to Khush, huddling into the warmth of his body.

The long, grey trunk reached out, and over his shoulders. For a moment, Tad thought Khush was going to push him away, but he didn't. Instead, he began to scoop up the dry leaves that lay under the bushes, dropping them on top of Tad until everything but his head was covered.

For a moment Tad puzzled about it, sleepily. But he was very tired, and it was cosy under the thick layer of leaves. Before five minutes had passed, he was asleep.

He was woken, in the thin light of morning, by a gentle tug on his earlobe. He opened his eyes slowly, frowning for a moment when he saw the interlacing branches above and felt the scratchy leaves against his bare skin.

The trunk that had tweaked his ear slapped him on the shoulder, urging him to his feet. When he looked round vaguely, Khush pushed him, as mothers push a stupid child.

Over there.

Tad staggered, got his balance, and looked.

Coming down from Parkersburg, alone on the wide river, was the flatboat. The blankets were strung out over it, hung up to dry, and Cissie was standing at the back, wrestling with the oar.

It was far too big for her. The boat moved erratically, sometimes in a zigzag and sometimes sideways on to the current, but she struggled determinedly, with her eyes fixed straight ahead, on the river in front of her.

Stark naked as he was, Tad raced to the end of the bar and began to caper up and down, waving his arms.

'Miss Cissie! Cissie! Here we are!'

She stared, dropped the sweep and only just caught it again before it went overboard. Then she started to try and turn the boat out of the current, towards the shore.

Tad knew she couldn't do it. It had taken all his strength to steer the boat in to shore each evening. Cissie must be crazy to be trying it on her own.

But then, she was crazy. She was drifting down the Ohio by herself, in a boat she couldn't control.

Tad went straight into the water, swimming for the front of the boat. In a few minutes, he was hauling himself up, wet and slippery as a fish. Snatching one of the hanging blankets, he draped it round his body and ran to Cissie.

'Here! Let me help!'

She didn't move. She just stared at him, with her mouth open.

Tad didn't waste time talking. He leaned against the sweep, to bring the boat round. Then he steered for the shore, reversing the oar as they drew near, to pole them into the shallows on the downstream side of the bar.

As they grounded safely, he whirled round in triumph. His whole body was warm and singing with the effort of steering.

'We did it! We got away! And we're together again!'

Cissie didn't answer. She just went on staring and staring, her eyes wide and her face stiff and expressionless.

'It's all right!' Tad said. 'Look, Cissie. It's all right.' Raising his head, he called into the trees. 'Come here!'

Khush ambled out of the undergrowth and began to walk towards Cissie, waving his trunk and squealing. Tad turned back, with a grin.

'You see? We're all safe.'

But Cissie didn't grin back. Her mouth shook. 'How *could* you?' she said.

'What do you mean?' Bewildered, Tad clutched the blanket tighter round his body. 'What have I done?'

'You let me think—you let me think that—'

But she couldn't get the words out. She choked to a stop, struggling for breath.

'I let you think *what?*' Tad couldn't understand why she wasn't shrieking with delight.

Cissie clenched her fists. 'You let me think you were dead. You went overboard, because of what I did, and then you just

77

disappeared. As if I hadn't had enough—'

'But I didn't mean—'

'*I thought I'd killed you as well!*'

'As well?'

For a second, the words hung in the air between them. Then, abruptly, Cissie turned and walked up the sandbank, into the trees.

I scarcely know how to write what happened yesterday.
My hand is shaking so hard that it is difficult to form the
letters.

Yesterday, people came out from Parkersburg to stop
us from proceeding and our boat was almost capsized.
Tad and Khush were flung out, and disappeared under
the water, and I was left alone, surrounded by boatloads
of people.

It was not my *fault*, Ketty, I swear it! But you may
imagine how I felt. To be saved once is a hard thing. To
be saved *twice*—

I nearly gave up my endeavour, then and there. It
would have been easy enough to stay in Parkersburg.
Three boatmen—thinking me to be a useful and hardy
boy—offered me employment on the spot, and four of
the good women of Parkersburg promised me board and
lodging for as long as I cared to have it.

I sat in the boat until it was quite dark, waiting for the
poor, drowned bodies to surface and debating what I
should do.

Dear Ketty, would you have wanted me, without
Khush? If I had come as a destitute orphan, would you
have taken me in?

Until that dreadful train journey, I would not have
hesitated about the answer. But now . . .

Because I would not leave my boat, the people around
towed it to the shore and hitched it there, swearing to
come back at dawn, to recommence the search.

Somewhat *before* dawn, I set sail secretly. I had not
planned what to do, but I knew that I had to keep my
freedom. I untied the boat and let the current draw me
out into the middle of the river and away towards the
west. A few minutes ago, I arrived at this sandbank,
where I now sit to write my letter.

And there, waiting for me, were Tad and Khush! No more harmed by the river than I was myself!

What a joyful reunion that should have been. Not only were all three of us preserved from death, but we were preserved IN SECRET. If we had simply escaped from the people of Parkersburg, they would, no doubt, have chased after us. But, as things are, they must imagine Tad and Khush to be drowned, and that will give us the chance to leave here unobserved.

But my hands are shaking, and I cannot think of anything except the train where Pa and Olivia died.

Chapter 13

Tad stood with the blanket round his shoulders for a long time, staring at the flatboat. At last, he walked slowly up into the trees, tugging at his makeshift cloak when it snagged on the branches.

Cissie was sitting in the hollow where he and Khush had slept. She was bent over a piece of paper, scribbling hard, and she didn't look up as Tad approached. She simply shielded her paper with her arm and went on writing.

Tad gathered up his damp clothes and went further into the trees to put them on. Then he walked back to the hollow.

'Miss Cissie—'

She didn't take any notice.

'Cissie—'

Very reluctantly, she lifted her head and blinked up at him. 'Yes?'

'What—?' *What should we do now?* That was what he meant to ask. But instead he said, 'Why don't you go to sleep? It's tiring, trying to steer the boat.'

'There's nothing wrong with me! I'm just fine!'

Khush rumbled uneasily at the tone of her voice and Tad reached out to pat his back leg. But he stepped sideways, out of reach, and flapped his ears.

'Khush?'

Tad forgot about Cissie for a moment. Turning to look at Khush, he saw that he was standing awkwardly, shifting from one foot to another and easing the weight off the leg Tad had tried to pat.

Suddenly, Tad heard Michael Keenan's voice in his head. *He has to be scrubbed every day, mind. Or we'll have a sick, unsavoury animal.* Since they left Pittsburgh, there had been no time to pick up the broom, except to scrub the bottom of the boat. Khush was clean enough now, after his swim in the

81

river, but the insides of his legs were inflamed. His feet must have been sore too, because he sidled away irritably when Tad tried to examine them.

Too much standing about in dirty, wet straw.

Cissie had gone back to her writing. Tad looked at her bent head. 'I think—'

'What?' she said shortly.

'We ought to stay here for a day or so. Khush needs a chance to heal up.'

'Don't be ridiculous.' Cissie rolled her papers up and crammed them into her trouser pocket. 'Someone's sure to see us if we wait around here.'

'But if we stay in the trees—'

'*We have to get to Nebraska.* We'll never do that if we don't keep going.'

Her voice was very high and determined. Tad nearly gave in, but then Khush moved away and he saw that he was limping slightly. Something had to be done.

He looked thoughtfully at the flatboat. 'If we stay here today, I can rig up another shelter, like the one Mr Nagel made. If no one sees Khush, they might go on thinking he was drowned last night.'

It wasn't much of a plan. Khush would probably wreck the new shelter as fast as the old one. But at least building it would give him some time. He could have a day to wander free, with dry, clean air round his legs.

Cissie considered. 'Maybe it's worth it,' she said grudgingly. 'Let's go and see if there are any saplings the right size.'

They pulled the boat up on to the sandbank and spent all day working on it, hardly speaking to each other. It took them all morning to cut down the trees and trim off their branches. Tad tested dozens of saplings for length and springiness before they began, and Cissie sighed impatiently.

'Do you have to fuss so? Why can't we just do it?'

'I must get the right ones.'

But he didn't judge as well as Mr Nagel. Two of the saplings they cut down were too short, and another one snapped when they tried to bend it to the right shape. By noon, Cissie was cross and sulky.

She carried off some bread and dried apple rings and sat by herself, in the hollow. Before Tad had finished, she was back by the boat, organizing Khush to drag the saplings on to the sand.

The work took them all day. They rigged the sapling arches exactly as Mr Nagel had done, but one of the tarpaulins had been thrown into the river when Tad and Khush went overboard at Parkersburg.

Tad went round to the front of the sandbank, to search among the debris brought down by the April flood water. But there was almost nothing from the flatboat. Only a tin mug and a single bottle of Michael Keenan's elephant tincture, glinting milky green among the battered branches and the scum of withered leaves.

Tad wiped the bottle clean, stared at it for a moment and put it in his pocket. Then he swilled out the mug and took it back to the flatboat. Instead of the lost tarpaulin, he used a patchwork of tattered blankets, nailed into place.

It was almost too dark to see by the time he knocked in the last nail. He put down the hammer and stepped back.

'There!'

'At last!' Cissie said. 'Now let's get back on the river!'

'Now?' Tad stared at her. He had been looking forward to some more food and a long sleep.

'Of course now,' said Cissie impatiently. 'We've already wasted a whole day.'

'But—' Tad swallowed hard. 'We can't go at night.'

'Don't be stupid. It was night when we started out.'

'But that was through the middle of Pittsburgh. They keep the river clear there. Here—'

Tad looked at the dark Ohio, whispering down past them with its invisible secrets. Rocks below the surface. Sandbanks. Tree-trunks under the water. Steamers that wouldn't see them. Coal tows. How could he make her understand?

'It's *dangerous*.'

'There's danger everywhere,' Cissie said fiercely. 'If God means us to get to Nebraska, we will. If not, all the cowardice in the world won't save us.'

'But—but we've hardly any food. Or fodder for Khush. And I haven't slept—'

Cissie ignored him. She simply walked off, so that his voice faded weakly into the air. When she came back, she was leading Khush, and she began to give him orders without even looking at Tad.

'Come here, Khush. Behind the boat. Now—HEAVE.'

Khush put his head down and threw all his weight against the wooden side. The boat started to slide towards the water.

'Cissie—' Tad said.

Khush looked up, and Cissie snapped at him. 'Heave!'

The boat slithered on to the wet mud.

'Cissie! Will you listen to me?'

'Heave!'

'Listen! Why do we have to hurry? No one's looking for us. They think Khush is drowned.'

'Heave!'

The boat slid halfway into the water. Cissie signalled to Khush to stop and then she rounded on Tad. 'I thought Mr Jackson was dead set on having Khush. Is he going to give up, just because someone tells him Khush is drowned?'

'He—' Tad remembered how Mr Jackson had spoken to Mr Nagel. *I bought that animal fair and square, and I'm going to get it back . . . the law is on my side . . .* He remembered the exact tone of voice, and the cold, menacing face. And he shivered. 'Maybe you're right.'

'Of course I'm right! He'll be down here, hunting for a body!'

'But he won't be here tonight—'

'You think we should sit about and wait for him?' Cissie turned away scornfully, grabbing the axe from the bottom of the boat. 'I'm going to cut some fodder.'

Tad started after her, set to go on arguing. But before he said a word, he saw that it was no use. If he argued, Cissie would simply go without him. She would load the fodder, take

Khush on board and pole herself into the Ohio, leaving him behind.

And she would drown, because she was too small to manage the heavy oar.

Grimly he began to gather up the greenery she was cutting and carry it on to the boat. But he didn't say a word. Not then. Not while Cissie coaxed Khush back on to the boat and into his new shelter. Not while he was poling the boat off the sandbank and into the channel.

He didn't speak until they were in midstream and he had pulled the oar round, so that they were facing forwards. Then he muttered, half under his breath, 'I still don't see why we have to leave tonight.'

Cissie looked up at him from where she was sitting, among the greenery.

'I need to be in Nebraska,' she hissed. '*I need Ketty.*'

She turned her back on him, gazing down river into the huge, moonless spread of black sky and black water.

For three days they travelled with the state of Ohio on the right bank and first West Virginia and then Kentucky on the left. But the state boundaries had no meaning. Day and night themselves had no meaning. The only thing that mattered was the dark, tumbling, treacherous water.

Tad tried to rest while it was light, because he had to. He gave the oar to Cissie, hoping she would manage to keep the boat straight, and he told her to wake him at the first sign of any danger. But he couldn't sleep.

His eyes, his brain—his whole body—were constantly tensed. Watching for rough water. Noticing which channel the other boats chose. Avoiding the steamers and all the traffic that went by constantly.

Waiting for Khush to break out.

At every hail from another boat, Khush shuffled and rumbled inside his tunnel of blankets. Cissie crooned to him all day long, and at night, when she was asleep, Tad took over the job. He leaned on the oar, scanning the dark water, and talked on and on, saying whatever came into his head.

'... a great, white house, with a cool porch for the middle of the day. And a garden, Khush. Ketty's garden. Shady trees and white flowers in the shadows ...'

The picture danced in the black air in front of him. Mysterious, swirling patterns of green. Khush snorted and champed in the dark, rocking against the sides of the boat.

It got harder and harder to keep him in the shelter. And that was hardly surprising. By the end of the second day, it smelt foul, and the fodder was almost finished.

But Cissie wouldn't hear of stopping.

'Not yet! We must get below Cincinnati first. That's halfway to the Mississippi. Then we can look for somewhere to land.'

'But Khush can't—'

'It's only eighty miles or so. It won't kill him, even if he has to go hungry for a day or so.'

'But—'

'Are *you* trying to give *me* orders?'

That was how all the arguments ended. Tad bit back the furious things he wanted to say and concentrated on the river, watching Khush's shelter out of the corner of his eye.

On the third day, it began to rain. From early in the morning, rain fell without stopping, soaking the boat and everything in it.

Tad cleaned it out as best he could while they were going along, but the space where Khush stood was encrusted with dirty straw. Now the straw and dung began to swirl round their feet, washing up against the corner where they had stacked what was left of their food.

Cissie baled hard, but by the middle of the afternoon things were unbearable. All three of them were cold and wet and hungry and Tad could see that Khush was on the verge of breaking out.

They had to get off the river. Very soon.

Towards the end of the day, a big coal tow came down river

behind them. Cissie was curled up on a heap of wet, bare branches, exhausted by baling. Tad glanced at her and saw that her eyes were closed.

He made up his mind.

He kept as close as he dared to the coal tow while it overtook him. Then, when its wash hit them, he turned the flatboat's bows suddenly left, towards the Kentucky shore.

The great wave of the wash carried them out of the current and into slack water. Carefully, without giving any sign to Cissie, Tad began to pole along the bank, towards a little wooded creek. If they could land there, they could rest and hide until the next morning.

Cissie was dozing. She didn't notice what he had done until they were nearly there. When she did, she jumped up and grabbed at the oar.

'You'll have us aground!'

'That's what I mean to do!' Tad wrenched the sweep out of her hands and thrust it down once more, driving the boat on to the mud. 'Can't you see what a state Khush is in?'

As they grounded, Khush trumpeted loudly and dragged at his tethers. His head appeared through the blankets at the far end of the shelter.

'Look at him!' Tad snapped. 'He's desperate to land!'

Cissie was about to snap back when she suddenly looked past him, up the creek. Tad turned round, to see what had caught her eye.

Two little girls, in brown holland dresses and blue pinafores, had come through the trees. They were standing very still, staring down at Khush.

The smaller girl squeaked, her voice carrying through the silence. 'Hannah! The elephant's here!'

The other girl nodded gravely and walked down the creek until she was beside the boat.

'We have been expecting you,' she said. 'Welcome to this Sojourning Place.'

Chapter 14

'IT'S A trap!' Cissie said, her voice rising to a shriek. 'You've steered us into a trap!'

Tad looked at the two little girls. They wore white linen caps, strange and old-fashioned, and heavy boots with wooden soles.

'Where are we?' he said.

'People call it Eastcote's Landing,' said the girl named Hannah. 'But, to us Strangers, it is the Sojourning Place.'

'And you knew we were coming?'

The little girl interrupted, coming forward excitedly. 'All men know, all along the river. A man and a woman came riding on horses, from Cincinnati.'

'Eliza! Thou must not say!' The bigger girl frowned childishly. 'The Abraham wishes to explain it himself.' She folded her hands and looked back at Tad and Cissie. 'We will take you to him.'

'Will you now?' Cissie flung her cropped head back defiantly. 'And why should we want to see your *Abraham*?'

The two girls looked horrified. They put their heads together and began to whisper.

'We have to go with them,' Tad muttered. 'If we try to sneak away now, they'll have a boat out after us.'

Cissie glared. 'You should have done what I told you to. If you hadn't stopped—'

'If I hadn't stopped, you would have been drowned dead in an hour or two,' Tad said sharply. 'Khush is still ready to wreck the boat.'

Cissie's mouth fell open. She didn't say a word. Just stepped back and let Tad untie Khush and take off the hobbling rope.

The moment his legs were free, Khush was out of the boat, moving stiffly towards the creek. The two strange girls circled warily round him, but he didn't take any notice. He was busy with the long, fresh grass and the tender shoots on the bushes.

Tad clambered out after him. As his feet touched the ground, Hannah bent to whisper something and Eliza, the little girl, ran off along the creek path.

'Springing the trap,' Cissie said sourly.

But she got out of the boat too, and stood fidgeting for twenty minutes, while Khush crammed food into his mouth.

Hannah didn't say anything. She waited, with her hands folded and her eyes lowered, watching Khush under her eyelids as he reached out and ripped at the bushes.

It was Cissie who broke the silence. 'If we *must* go, let's go now!' She smacked Khush's leg. 'Move up there! We've got an Abraham to meet.'

She would not speak to Tad as they walked up the creek path behind Hannah. It ran for almost a mile, winding through woods and round little hills, and she stumped all the way without a glance at the country they were passing through.

Tad peered round, trying to make sense of the place. He could see that the woods were tended. Neat piles of logs were stacked at intervals along the path, and the trees had been cut to a pattern, leaving stumps for new coppice wood to grow. But they did not pass any houses, and there was no sign of boundaries between one farm and another.

The town ahead stayed hidden until the last moment. The final twist of the path brought them round the shoulder of a hill, so that they were suddenly on the edge of a group of buildings.

Cissie stopped, with Khush beside her. 'Strangest town *I* ever saw.'

Tad nodded. He had expected a huddle of little wooden houses. A couple of stores. Maybe a hotel. But what he saw was a square of fine frame buildings, two storeys high, set at the entrance to a wide valley. The centre of the square was a herb garden, laid out in neat, rectangular beds, and beyond lay two large barns and a patchwork of little, hedged fields.

On the path round the herb garden was a double row of men and women in plain, dark clothes. Fifty or sixty of them, standing very still, with their hands folded. As Hannah led the way into the square, the row parted, leaving a clear path to the centre.

'The whole town's come to take a look at us,' Tad muttered.

'They haven't come to look,' Cissie hissed. 'They've come to grab us!'

For a split second, eerily, Tad remembered Markle. There, too, everyone had turned out to see the elephant. But the place had been full of excitement and colour and shouting. Here, there was no sound except the noise of their own feet, crunching on the cinder paths between the beds of herbs.

On the far side of the square was an old man who stood with both hands resting on a stick. His back was humped and twisted and he was no taller than Cissie, but the other men and women turned towards him as Khush appeared.

The old man walked slowly forward into the middle of the garden, his bright eyes watching all of them. Then he bobbed his head to Cissie and Tad.

'Good evening. I am Francis Eastcote, the Abraham of this Sojourning Place. I must tell you that you are not welcome here. We have prayed long and hard for you to land somewhere else.'

'We don't want to be here either.' Cissie stood very straight, looking fiercely at him. 'Why don't we just go away?'

Tad heard the whisper of disapproval that ran round the square. But the old man's expression did not change.

'You cannot avoid God's hand. He brought you to this place for some reason, and if you try to escape you will certainly be captured. The whole river is watching out for the elephant, from here to Cincinnati.'

Cissie screwed up her fists. 'Mr Jackson's been very thorough,' she muttered to Tad. 'I *knew* he wouldn't give up.'

The old man smiled wryly. 'I do not think it is in Mr Jackson's nature to give up. He came here, with a receipt, to show that the elephant belonged to him, and he was—very fierce.'

'I told you how it would be!' Cissie hissed. 'He must have

jumped on a train, as soon as he heard from Parkersburg.' She turned to Mr Eastcote. 'That receipt is forged! The elephant's mine. My father would never have sold him for so little. Ask Tad.'

Mr Eastcote's eyes swivelled round. They were large and compelling, and of a strange, light hazel colour. 'You are Tad?'

Tad looked down at his fingers. 'There's no point in telling you anything,' he said slowly. 'If you've heard Mr Jackson's story, you'll have made up your mind. You won't listen to what we say, even if it is the truth.'

Cissie snorted impatiently, but Mr Eastcote's eyes stayed steady. 'Thou does not know the ways of this Place, young man. It is not our custom to trust to our own wisdom. We enquire closely into all things and then lay them in the hands of God. He leads us, as he led our fathers to this Place.'

'Alleluia,' muttered all the people round the square.

'Alleluia,' Mr Eastcote answered, rather absently. He stepped back, and waved a hand at the building behind him. 'This evening we shall talk, and you can stay here tonight.'

Cissie's eyes narrowed. 'How do we know you won't send for Mr Jackson, while we're asleep?'

There was another ripple of disapproval, but Cissie didn't care. She lifted her head and glared at Mr Eastcote. And he looked straight back at her, suddenly smiling.

'If I wanted to send for Mr Jackson, I could do it now.'

'So what *are* you going to do?' Cissie said grudgingly.

'We are going to listen to you,' Mr Eastcote said. 'You may put the elephant in the Old Barn. What does he need?'

Tad answered, without waiting for Cissie to speak. 'Lots of food, if you can spare it. Hay and roots and greenstuff. And water. And if you have any oil—'

'One of the Brothers shall bring it to you.' Mr Eastcote turned to Cissie and looked steadily at her for a moment or two. Then he beckoned the two girls who had met them down by the creek.

'Hannah. Eliza. Take our visitor into the Children's House, and find her some more suitable clothes.'

91

The girls looked puzzled. Then they realized what he meant. Their mouths fell open, and one or two of the other children giggled behind their hands. Cissie turned a dull, angry red.

'I don't want to change my clothes. I like to dress like this.'

'It is not the custom here for girls to wear boys' clothes,' Mr Eastcote said calmly. 'Our Sisters dress modestly, according to the word of God.'

He signalled to Hannah and Eliza and they caught Cissie's arms and began to hustle her away to the building on the left. Khush took a step after her.

'No, Khush.' Tad laid a hand on his side. 'Stay here.'

He felt Khush's trunk come sliding over his shoulder and he leaned his cheek against its grey folds.

'Eli will take thee to the barn,' Mr Eastcote said.

Another old man stepped out of the row and Tad followed him slowly into the shadows of a great wooden barn. He did not need to give any orders. Khush followed unbidden, with his trunk still looped lightly round Tad's neck.

Eastcote's Landing
(alias The Sojourning Place)
20th April

For the time being, we are no longer afloat, but in the
oddest place I ever visited. You cannot imagine how
peculiar it is, dear Ketty.

We have fallen among Strangers. They belong to a
sect dedicated, so far as I can see, to the principle that
God put us on this Earth to be meek and wear
homespun.

All the grown people—men and women alike—are
subservient to a shrivelled old man, like a monkey,
whom they call 'The Abraham'. (Although they treat
him as if he were a much more Important Person.)

The divine monkey's predecessor, some hundred years
ago, gathered together a band of thieves, converted
them to homespun righteousness and led them out of
England and into this valley in Kentucky. He promised
them riches and freedom and these—their descendants
believe—they now enjoy. Although how that can be so,
when they dwell in wooden huts and obey orders, is
more than I can understand.

The simian wisdom is that pride and greed and theft—
and all great sins—are the result of owning private
property. Accordingly, the Strangers hold all things in
common and each one works for the general good, their
actions being governed in every respect by the Direct
Guidance of God.

Or so I am informed by the two girls who have been
appointed my keepers—and wardrobe mistresses.

In my case, the Direct Guidance of God is that I must
not wear breeches. So I have laid aside my boy's disguise
to become a Stranger Sister, dressed in brown, with a
linen cap upon my head. Already I feel an amazing
meekness, and an urge to soften my voice and lower my
eyes.

Tomorrow I must plead for my right to travel on towards you, instead of being handed over to the *unconverted* thief who has followed us from Pittsburgh, chasing what he pretends is his private property.

I shall plead hard, do not fear. I have no wish to stay longer in this place, with its talk of *sin* and *guilt* and *retribution*. I want to come to you—bringing Khush with me—and make a *fresh start*.

CHAPTER 15

THE NEXT time Tad saw Cissie, he didn't recognize her. She walked into supper with four other girls, dressed exactly like them, in a plain, heavy dress and a dark blue pinafore. Her wooden soles clacked as she followed them across to the children's table.

With the Stranger clothes, she had put on different manners. She kept her head lowered, whispering sideways to Hannah and Eliza. The white linen cap hid her cropped hair and its shadow fell over her face.

Tad felt alone and awkward as he sat down beside two little boys. He had washed for the meal, but his clothes—his only clothes—were spattered with dirty water and oil, from cleaning Khush. He wanted to apologize for the state of them, but there seemed no way to do it.

The meal was eaten in silence. Even the boys who sat round Tad didn't say a word, although they looked at him constantly. He could tell that their heads were full of questions about Khush, but not one of them spoke.

Tad had barely finished his bean stew and bread when Mr Eastcote stood up and nodded across at the children's table. It was obviously a signal. Immediately, all the Stranger children stood up and began to clear away the plates and dishes.

Cissie started to help, but Mr Eastcote stopped her, with a lifted hand.

'Not thee, Sister. Thou must stay here, to take part in our Congregation.'

All round the room, there was an expectant rustling. Tad thought, at first, that the Strangers were interested to hear what he and Cissie had to say, but no one looked towards them. The eagerness was for the Congregation itself.

The moment the tables were clear, they were carried to the

end of the long room, and the children left. Someone closed the doors and the Strangers carried their chairs into the centre, to form one large circle.

Mr Eastcote's chair was set down first, at the head of the circle, facing the door. He waited until everyone was sitting and then he beckoned to Tad and Cissie.

'It is time for you to speak. You may be sure that we shall listen very closely.'

More than a hundred eyes fixed themselves on Tad as he walked across the circle to stand beside Mr Eastcote's chair. Cissie came from opposite to join him, moving with small, unfamiliar steps.

Mr Eastcote stood up and instantly the room was silent.

'Brothers and Sisters,' he said, 'we are God's Congregation, sojourning here on earth as strangers and pilgrims. May we hear with His ears and give voice to His will.'

All together, the Strangers answered. 'May He grant thee wisdom to understand His will, O Abraham.'

It must have been what they always said, but it was no mechanical response. Each person spoke with particular and fervent emphasis, and the air was electric with concentration.

Mr Eastcote sat down. 'Now!'

The vibrant stillness bore in on Tad so that he could hardly breathe. With enormous effort, he forced out one word.

'Cissie—'

Cissie was ready. She stood with her head lowered, but her voice came steady and clear from under the white cap.

'You think we are thieves. But I am not a thief. Nor is Tad. We are orphans now, but our dead parents brought us up in the strictest honesty.'

Her words dropped into the stillness like rocks into a level lake. No one moved, but Tad felt the ripples spread across the room. He kept his face blank, wondering what she meant to say.

She glanced up quickly, and then lowered her eyes again. 'It's easy for things to take on the wrong appearance. And once someone is branded a thief, no one will give him a fair hearing.'

Mr Eastcote's eyes sharpened. 'Thou will have a fair hearing here,' he said, with a touch of acid in his voice. 'There is no need for anything but the plain truth.'

Cissie gave him one quick glance. Then she straightened and spoke more briskly. 'Khush—the elephant—belonged to my father. My father and my sister and I travelled up and down the east coast, giving elephant shows for our living. Until—'

She clenched her fists, but her voice did not waver.

'—until a few days ago, when Pa and Olivia were killed in a railroad accident outside Pittsburgh. By the mercy of God—'

Her hands unclenched and twisted together, turning until they blotched red and white. But she went on speaking.

'—I was flung out of the window, and lived. But all Pa's money was burnt with him. I had nothing except Khush. And then Mr Jackson appeared—'

This time, she did falter. Her voice stopped and she looked down, drawing a long, deep breath. One of the Sisters prompted her.

'Thou did not know thy father had sold the elephant?'

'He didn't sell him!' Cissie flung up her head, so violently that the white cap tumbled off. Underneath, her face was blazing. 'Mr Jackson's receipt is forged! Pa had no call to sell Khush for—for *nothing*. And he never wrote in black ink!'

For one uncomfortable moment, Tad remembered that she had never actually seen the receipt. Then, like everyone else in the room, he was swept along by her fervour and her fury.

Like almost everyone. Mr Eastcote's expression did not change. 'Maybe this is the truth,' he said drily. 'But we have only thy word against Mr Jackson's.'

'Ask Tad!'

All the eyes moved to Tad's face and he gulped, turning pink.

'Don't know much about it,' he muttered awkwardly. 'Only that Mr Jackson offered five hundred dollars before, and Mr Keenan said it was an insult. And—and—' The rest of the words came out in a rush. 'Seems very odd that when Mr Keenan's alive there's no selling the elephant, and the moment he's dead someone pops up with a paper that says he did it after all.'

Some of the Strangers nodded and glanced at each other, but Mr Eastcote's face was stern.

'Odd, but not illegal,' he said. 'The receipt—unless it can be *proved* false—puts the law on Mr Jackson's side. He is a man who will use every weapon that he has, and we Strangers must be careful of quarrels about property. Because we do not seek to lay up treasures for ourselves, people suspect us of wishing to steal theirs.'

Cissie folded her arms and stared stubbornly across the room. 'You will be stealing mine, if you give Khush to Mr Jackson.'

'What does thy friend say?' Mr Eastcote's eyes moved suddenly to Tad, and all the eyes in the room followed them. He was skewered by stares from every side.

'Seems—seems like the elephant *ought* to belong to Miss Cissie,' he stuttered.

The hazel eyes stared harder. 'But?'

Tad shuffled awkwardly, aware that Cissie was glaring at him, but he couldn't look away from Mr Eastcote's eyes. They transfixed him, and as he stared into them he thought of Khush. Thought of him so vividly that he might have been present there, in the centre of the circle.

'It doesn't make sense,' he said slowly. 'How can an elephant, like Khush, belong to a person? There isn't one of us could stop him, if he chose to make off. Cissie and I couldn't keep him prisoner against his will. While we were coming down the river, he could have run away a thousand times. But he—he—'

Tad fumbled. Then he found himself saying words he had never even thought.

'He comes with us, but he *belongs* to himself.'

He heard his own voice and turned scarlet with miserable embarrassment. How could an animal belong to itself? That was ridiculous.

But Cissie pounced on the idea. 'There's the answer to your problem! Let Khush choose! I'll get on the boat, without

98

giving him any orders. If he follows, he's mine. If not, you can send a messenger to Mr Jackson.'

There was a moment's silence, while the Strangers whispered, in little groups. Then Mr Eastcote stood up.

'Brothers and Sisters, let us put this in the hands of God. Let us struggle diligently to discover His will.'

He rose from his chair and walked into the middle of the room and the Strangers stood up and formed a ring round him, with their arms linked and their eyes closed.

For a moment, all of them were completely still. Then, as Tad and Cissie glanced at each other, wondering what was going to happen, the humming began.

At first it was steady, a low-pitched hum that rose from the whole circle on one, unbroken note. But gradually it took on a throbbing rhythm, pulsing louder and softer at the speed of a beating heart. And the circle began to move in time to the pulse.

For ten minutes or more, people simply swayed from side to side. Then the pace increased, and the circle started to shuffle round, with slow side-steps.

Then faster steps.

And faster and faster.

The humming and the steps quickened together, rising gradually to a relentless crescendo. Only Mr Eastcote, in the very centre, was motionless. Around him, the circle spun impossibly fast, old and young whirling together until Tad thought they must surely lose their footing and tumble into a great heap on the floor. He and Cissie shrank back, among the tables, and stared with their mouths open.

Then the circle split apart. People wrenched their arms free and spun separately, or dropped to their knees and buried their faces in their hands. And still the humming throbbed on, drowning out all other sounds, all possibility of thinking.

Or so it seemed to Tad. But then, below the humming, he heard words. At first they were indistinguishable, but the same words were repeated over and over again, in different parts of the room, and slowly he made out what they were.

Let the elephant choose.

Over and over again they came, until they beat with their own rhythm, first from one side and then from the other, rising above the humming.

Let the elephant choose.

Cissie glanced at Tad and smiled, very faintly.

The words and the humming beat against each other until the whole room rang with the rhythm and counter-rhythm. One by one, the exhausted Strangers began to drop to their knees.

Then, slowly, the words faded back into humming and the humming dwindled to a thread of sound. At last, it died away completely, until there was nothing to be heard but the breathing of dozens of people, kneeling all over the room.

For ten or fifteen minutes, no one moved. Then Mr Eastcote walked out of the centre and over to his chair. He sat down, hands folded, and the other Strangers followed him, in ones and twos. But it was another half hour before the last man heaved himself from the floor.

When they were all seated again, Mr Eastcote looked round. 'Brothers and Sisters, we have heard the will of God.'

'Praise Him for His guidance!' said the Strangers.

They were all smiling. Exultant. Tad stared round the circle, dazed by their radiant faces, but Cissie was itching to speak. As soon as there was silence, she stepped forward triumphantly. 'Give me my own clothes, and we'll go now. You won't be troubled any more.'

Too simple, thought Tad, watching Mr Eastcote's face. The hazel eyes were sharp.

'If you go now, we shall certainly be troubled,' Mr Eastcote said. 'You will be caught at the next place down the river, and you have a relentless enemy. He will make you suffer, and the Strangers will suffer too.'

'But I thought you had decided—'

'And so we have.' Mr Eastcote was very calm. 'The Brothers and Sisters have discovered the will of God. But it is for the Abraham to say how that shall be brought about safely.'

'But—'

'Sit down, Sister, and listen to me.'

Tad grabbed Cissie's arm and pulled her into a chair and Mr Eastcote folded his hands.

'God will show us a way for you to escape,' he said gravely. 'You need to travel on a boat where you can hide. And *we* need a boat whose captain we can trust.'

From across the room came a single, whispered word.

'*Jedediah.*'

That was all. But the Brothers and Sisters sat up straighter, and Mr Eastcote nodded.

'Maybe.' He looked at Cissie and Tad. 'Wait here for a few days. We will hide you. And then, if all goes well, we will send you down the river. All the way to Cairo, if you like.'

'And Khush?' Cissie said quickly.

For a split second, Mr Eastcote hesitated, and some of the Strangers glanced at each other. Tad noticed, but Cissie was concentrating on her question.

'Will Khush be able to travel on this boat of yours?'

Mr Eastcote lifted his head and looked straight into her eyes. 'If the elephant wants to go with you, there will be room for him too.'

CHAPTER 16

FOR A week they waited at Eastcote's Landing, not knowing what they waited for.

Cissie spent the time in the laundry, stirring huge coppers full of boiling water and spreading sheets on the long wooden drying racks in the loft. Tad never saw her, except at mealtimes, when she filed in between Hannah and Eliza. She sat near him, demure in her white cap and smelling of soap, but he had no chance to talk to her.

Tad was always busy in the Old Barn. He carried food and water for Khush, scrubbed him and oiled his skin. And, above all, he kept him inside the barn, hidden away from visitors.

There were always visitors at Eastcote's Landing. Regular rivermen called in for meals. Neighbours dropped by to order leather horse-harness, or the fine, embroidered babyclothes that the Sisters made. And steamboat passengers stopped off because they were curious to see the Strangers.

Whenever anyone was there, Tad sat in the barn, talking to Khush.

'Not much longer now. When we get to Nebraska, you'll have the whole wide prairie to roam over. And Ketty will be there . . . '

Squatting in the dim barn, surrounded by sweet, dusty hay, he dreamt of Ketty's summer garden. Trees drooping over white lilies. The heavy smell of tangled roses. And the intricate dappling of a hundred shades of green . . .

He pulled the bottle of tincture from his pocket and tilted it into the light. The liquid swirled mysteriously, suggesting something beyond his imaginings. Even when Khush lowered his head and ate calmly, he let his voice drift on, staring deep into the streaked green shadows.

On the seventh day, the coal tow came.

Tad knew, from the moment he woke and came out of the barn, that something different was expected. There was no more noise than usual, but everywhere there were faces at windows, and some of the Sisters crossed the central square a dozen times before midday.

It was almost twilight when the young men came. They marched up from the river just as the evening meal was ready. Tall, brown-skinned men, dressed like any other crew from a coal tow, but moving with the quiet ease of the Strangers. Tad stood in the doorway of the barn and watched them come.

There was someone to greet each one of them, and Tad could see the resemblances. Mother and son. Father and son. Sister and brother. But he was surprised when Mr Eastcote beckoned him across to meet one of them.

'This is the man thou has been waiting for, Tad. My son, Jedediah.'

'Good-day,' said Jedediah.

No resemblance there. He was very tall and strongly built, with hair as black as Mr Eastcote's was white. Only his eyes had something of the same steadiness.

'Not all our young men choose to stay in the Sojourning Place,' Mr Eastcote said. 'But they are still Strangers in their hearts. I have asked Jedediah to help you.'

Gravely, Jedediah looked down at Tad. 'I hear thou has a special cargo to be shipped. May I see?'

They turned towards the Old Barn and Jedediah looked round to gather his crew. By the time Tad lifted the heavy wooden bar from the barn door, all the men were there.

He pushed the door open. For a second, the inside was just a blur of shadows. Then, as their eyes adjusted to the light, they saw Khush raise his head.

'Praise Him for His wondrous works,' Jedediah said softly. He was staring at Khush with a smile of astonished delight, like a child seeing an old story come true.

Then, with a clatter of wooden soles, Cissie came flying out of the laundry. She ran straight across to the barn. To Jedediah.

'You're the one! Hannah told me! Are you going to take us to Cairo?'

Jedediah smiled down at her wide eyes and her narrow face, half-hidden by the linen cap. 'Thou looks at home here, Sister. Why does thou want to go to a place like Cairo?'

'I'm travelling west,' Cissie said, squaring her shoulders and lifting her chin. 'With my elephant.'

'*Thy* elephant?' Jedediah smiled a gentle, teasing smile. 'Can a little Sister like thee own a great creature like that?'

Cissie didn't answer him directly. Instead, she marched into the barn, until she was only a few feet away from Khush. Then she spoke abruptly, without any introduction.

'*But still I have not revealed the most amazing fact about Khush—*'

It was Michael Keenan's voice, an octave higher. The same showman's flourish. The same flamboyant, dramatic tone. But when—?

Tad was too slow chasing the memory. He gasped with the rest when Khush reached out his trunk, snatched Cissie off the floor of the barn and swung her high into the air.

But this time she had no crutches to drop, and she did not pretend to faint. Instead, she looked down triumphantly, kicking her legs in a flurry of white frills and scarlet ribbons.

'He's *my* elephant! And when I leave here, he will follow me!'

The crew laughed, but Jedediah glanced uncertainly at his father.

'God's purpose will be revealed,' Mr Eastcote said firmly. 'We wait in faith.'

Immediately after supper, the Stranger Brothers went down to the landing with Jedediah's crew, but no one told Tad and Cissie why. They were simply set to pack their things.

'And then sleep,' said Mr Eastcote. 'I will wake you when we are ready.'

They bundled up what was left in the flatboat and stacked it in the barn. Then they worked at gathering food for Khush. The Stranger Sisters gave them bread and bacon for themselves, and brought back Cissie's boys' clothes, washed and mended. They laughed when she offered them money.

'Thou has paid already,' one of them said. She lifted Cissie's hand and ran her finger over the water-wrinkled fingertips. 'There is no need for any more.'

By the time Mr Eastcote reappeared, everything was ready. He pushed the barn door open and stood outside in the dark, holding his lantern high. Cissie lifted two of the bundles to sling them over Khush's back.

'No.' Mr Eastcote held up a hand. 'He must be free not to go with you. You must carry your own baggage.'

Cissie shrugged and swung the bundles over her shoulder, waiting for Tad to pick up what he could carry.

'I'm going now,' she said, without looking at Khush.

It wasn't a familiar command, but Tad could see that Khush knew what was going on. He raised his head and looked from Tad to Cissie and then down at the rest of the bundles. When they started to move, he followed them out of the barn. Cissie grinned cheekily sideways at Mr Eastcote, but Tad didn't think it would be so easy. There was going to be some kind of test.

They didn't take the path down to the creek where they had come ashore. Instead, they headed further downstream, to the Strangers' jetty.

The coal tow was moored in the dark, at the far end, an enormous island of shadow, rising just above the level of the water. Huge barges, lashed together to make a platform more than five hundred feet long. At the back was a tall steamboat, fired up and ready to go, its smokestack belching sparks into the black sky.

Tad stared. How could Khush travel secretly on a coal tow? If he stood on the barges, he would be visible for miles. And if there was room for him on the steamboat, it could only be on the open deck, where everyone that passed could see him clearly.

They walked down the jetty, their feet echoing on the boards. As they drew level with the barges, Mr Eastcote lifted his lantern.

'This is where you will travel. It will be completely secret.'

Cissie gasped. 'Khush won't go in there!'

Tad stood and looked where Mr Eastcote was pointing. Into a deep, black hole. One of the coal barges had been mined. All the coal from the centre had been taken out, to leave a square pit, with the sides boarded.

It was big enough even for Khush. Twenty feet by eight, and ten feet deep, with a smell that took Tad straight back to Markle. To coal dust that silted into his hair, and up his nose, and between his teeth.

The smell of despair.

He looked at the hole. 'It's impossible for Khush to get in there. He can't jump straight down, like a cat. And if he did, he'd break the bottom of the barge.'

'It will not be impossible,' Mr Eastcote said gravely. 'We are going to make a ramp. The Brothers are bringing the rest of the wood from your boat.'

'But—Khush won't go in there!' Cissie clenched her fists. 'You've tricked us!'

Jedediah glanced at his father, but Mr Eastcote's eyes did not leave Cissie's face. 'We have put ourselves into the hands of God. To Him, all things are possible. If He wishes the elephant to go with you, He will convey him into the belly of the coal barge. As once He conveyed Jonah into the belly of the whale. Do you doubt His power?'

'But it's not fair!' Cissie said furiously. She whirled round and looked pleadingly at Jedediah. '*You* don't think it's a fair test, do you?'

For a split second, Jedediah hesitated. Then Mr Eastcote turned to look at him, and he shook his head sadly at Cissie.

'My father is the Abraham of this Place. It is for him to say how things shall be done.'

'But—'

Cissie was scarlet and she looked ready to go on arguing. Tad pulled her out of the way before she could say any more.

'We can't complain,' he hissed. 'It's what we agreed to.'

'No, we didn't,' she muttered sulkily. But she turned away from Mr Eastcote and stood silently, watching some of the Brothers carrying long planks up the jetty, while others brought sacks full of roots and handed them into the hole.

Tad was very close to Khush. He reached sideways, in the dark, and ran his hand slowly over the soft skin of the elephant's side, stroking it over and over again in a steady rhythm.

When the ramp was built, and the fodder was neatly stacked, Mr Eastcote beckoned to Tad and Cissie. 'You must go in without speaking. If you give any orders to the elephant, he is not free to choose.'

Cissie frowned. Tad knew she was trying to think of a way to cheat, but she couldn't give a command without speaking. She picked up her bundles and stepped on to the barge.

Tad followed, looking back at Khush. Even in the lantern light, he could see the strange, sideways set of the elephant's head. Khush was puzzled, and his trunk was twitching, because he hated the smell of the barges.

Tad and Cissie scrambled over the surface of the coal and then walked down the ramp, into the pit. After the first few steps, everything was hidden, except the black sky above and the boards below, that held back the coal.

They heard Khush rattle his trunk and shuffle his feet, but they couldn't see him.

It was two or three minutes before anyone spoke. Then, quite softly, Mr Eastcote said, 'I do not think the elephant will come with you. He has not taken one step towards the barge.'

'It's not fair!' Cissie said bitterly. 'You cheated!'

'Thou suggested the test.' Mr Eastcote's voice turned colder. 'He could have followed. And he has refused.'

'But—'

Cissie gulped, and Tad realized that there was no more time. Another minute, and they would have lost Khush.

Raising his voice, he spoke from the bottom of the pit. He said the only thing he could think of, and he said it very slowly and loudly, so that Khush knew where he was.

107

'You must show him that we're going. He's never seen us travel in this boat before. He has to understand.'

'What does thou want us to do?' Jedediah said quickly. His voice was much gentler.

It was a gamble, but Tad couldn't think of any alternative. He took a deep breath.

'Cast off the mooring ropes. And hold the lantern high, so that Khush can see you untie them.'

'No!' Cissie hissed.

But only Tad heard. She grabbed his arm and stood very still, listening as Jedediah gave the order.

There were four mooring ropes. The shadows in the pit shifted as the lantern lit up the first. Tad heard the shuffle of rope sliding out of its knot and the soft flop as it was thrown up on to a barge.

One.

And no sound from Khush.

The lantern moved again, to the second rope. There was a shuffle on the jetty and its timbers creaked, but no one said anything. Another rope slapped aboard.

Two.

Cissie's fingers dug into Tad's arm as the third rope was loosened. Even before it was flung up, they felt the great island of barges sway with the movement of the river.

Three.

'Last one now,' Jedediah said, very softly.

The lantern moved sideways again—and there was a loud, abrupt noise. A frightened, protesting trumpeting. Water slopped suddenly round the side of the barge as it dipped towards the jetty.

'Khush!' Cissie and Tad scrambled up the ramp until their heads rose above the level of the coal. Khush had stepped on to the barge. Delicately, lifting each foot and placing it with care, he was picking his way towards them. And Jedediah was close behind.

'Talk him steady,' he said. 'Or he'll have half the coal in the water.'

It didn't occur to Tad to wait for Cissie. He began to croon in the soothing voice he had been using for the last week. 'Come here, Khush. Steady now. Come here.'

Inch by inch, step by step, Khush moved towards them over the coal. When he reached the top of the ramp, he hesitated for a second, looking down. But it was only for a second. Then Jedediah held the lantern high and he stepped on to the ramp, testing the planks carefully before he put his weight on them.

Jedediah held the lantern up until they were all safely in the bottom of the barge. Then he said, 'We have seen the will of God. Alleluia!'

There was a hint of challenge in his voice, but Mr Eastcote rose to it. His reply came from the jetty, strong and certain.

'To Him, all things are possible. Alleluia!'

For a second, Jedediah stood in the patch of light above the pit, grinning down at Tad and Cissie. Then he began to slide planks across the hole.

The planks were covered with tarpaulins and, when those were on, lumps of coal rattled across the surface. By the time the work was done, Tad guessed that their barge must look the same as all the others. They were completely shut in, with only a couple of narrow cracks between the tarpaulins.

Then the lantern moved away, and they were in total darkness. Tad leaned his head sideways, resting it against Khush's shoulder. What would it have been like to hear the fourth rope thrown up on to the tow? To feel the barges moving off down the river, leaving Khush on the jetty?

His face twisted and the air caught in his throat. For a second, he could hardly breathe.

In the Dark and surrounded by Coal
27th April

Pa used to frighten Olivia and me with stories of the old slave ships. He sat by the fire, in the dark, and talked about the cramped, crowded decks and the inhuman treatment until we could almost imagine ourselves there, squeezed into a hole with other bodies all around us.

Well, now I know what it was that he left out of his descriptions—the smell.

I am penned into a narrow, secret room in the depths of a coal barge, sharing my space with a great, rough boy and an elephant. The closeness and the lack of privacy are all that Pa told us of, but the smell outweighs all those. Even now, after only a few hours, it is unpleasant. It is not hard to guess how much worse it will be, when we have spent days in this place.

There is no way of keeping clean, however hard we try, and no escape from the foul air. The only ventilation is this narrow gap in the tarpaulins, by which I crouch, taking advantage of the light to write to you.

Do you think that God wipes out our sins if we suffer here on earth?

CHAPTER 17

TAD KNEW they had been travelling for hours, because his voice was hoarse. Ever since they left Eastcote's Landing, he had been sitting in the dark, murmuring to Khush, to keep him calm.

'You'll have room to move, on the prairie. As much room as you want. And long, fresh grass . . . '

He was imagining it for himself, as much as for Khush.

' . . . and Ketty will be there in her garden, in the shade of the apple trees. The green, green shade . . . '

He could hear Khush tugging at the food that the Strangers had stacked in the corner for him. Tugging and chewing and shuffling from one foot to another. Once or twice he knocked against the bucket, and once or twice he lifted his trunk and blew gently into Tad's face, but for most of the time he chewed.

Cissie was sitting at the top of the ramp, writing on her bundle of paper. She blocked the tiny gap that Jedediah had left to give them light, but Tad didn't like to ask her to move. He screwed up his eyes, to make himself forget the dark, and concentrated on the pictures in his head.

' . . . rich, wide farmland. Enough for everyone that comes. A new start, in a new state . . . '

But he couldn't keep it up for ever. His throat grew sore, his voice got hoarser and he started to cough.

'Be quiet!' The darkness shifted as Cissie turned on the ramp. 'We're coming up to Cincinnati. You can't cough now.'

Tad held his breath, almost choking, and then coughed again. 'I can't be—quiet—someone has to talk—to Khush.'

Cissie sighed, but she pushed her papers into her trouser pocket and scrambled down the ramp. 'I can do it for a little while. Go up there and get a breath of air. *But don't cough.*'

Khush was already rumbling irritably, because Tad's chant-

111

ing had stopped. As Cissie sat down on the bundles, he tweaked her hair, and she smacked his trunk away.

'Behave yourself! Do you want Ketty to hear you've been bad? She likes good, gentle elephants . . . '

She settled down into her own chant, and Khush quietened down and began to eat again. Tad crawled up the ramp.

When he reached the top, the fresh air hit him like cold water, and the early morning sunlight blared through the gap in the tarpaulins. Crouching down, he put his eye to it.

The raft of coal barges stretched all around, like a huge plain, scattered with great, black rocks. Beyond the rocks, distant and tiny, was the Cincinnati waterfront.

Tall, frilled steamboat funnels crowded along the bank, half-hidden by the early-morning mist. Behind them, the buildings sat cupped in a curve of hills. They hung like the walls of an imagined kingdom, between the river mist below and the smoky sky above.

Out of the mist, faint sounds of early-morning bustle floated over the water to Tad. Shouting voices. The clatter and scrape of horses' hoofs. And the dip and scurry of battered little harbour craft around the great steamboats.

Keeping the main channel, the coal tow moved steadily down river, under one bridge and on towards a second. Tad's eyes flickered first one way and then another as he tried to take in all that was going on.

But he missed the rowboat. It came suddenly out of the mist, just on the other side of the coal barges. He glimpsed it for an instant, as it bobbed across his line of vision, and then it was close against the steamboat, too low for him to see.

But in that instant, he had glimpsed a bonnet trimmed with purple feathers. And it was Mr Jackson's voice that hailed the coal tow.

'Good morning! Have you seen an elephant on your way down the river?'

Tad gripped the edge of the tarpaulin. They were there, then. He and Cissie had travelled hundreds of miles, and it had made no difference at all. Mr Jackson and Esther were still close behind them. He felt his hands begin to shake.

I bought that elephant, fair and square, and I'm going to get it back . . . the law is on my side.

They would never get past those two. How could they slip by, undetected, when the rowboat was almost near enough to touch?

But Jedediah's crew answered cheerfully, their voices carrying across the coal to Tad.

'How did thou lose an *elephant?*'

'I saw a hippopotamus once, in Philadelphia.'

'Maybe the crocodiles have eaten it?'

A loud, angry sigh came from the rowboat. Tad could imagine exactly how Esther must look.

'If I have to listen to those tired old jokes once more, I shall EXPIRE!'

That was what she always said. *If I have to clear up another crumb of broken crockery, Tad Hawkins . . . if I have to explain that again . . . if I have to send you back to scrub that floor once more . . . I shall EXPIRE.* For a second, as Tad crouched there in the darkness, with the smell of coal dust in his nostrils, he might have been back in Markle. He shuddered, and ground his knuckles together.

But Jedediah answered calmly. 'We have seen no elephant in any of the boats we have passed, ma'am. And no strange animal walking along either bank.'

It was the exact, careful truth. To Tad, the missing pieces seemed to shout out loud, and he hunched lower under the tarpaulin, waiting for Esther to shriek and for Mr Jackson's heavy tread to come slowly towards him over the coal.

But it didn't happen. They obviously thought they had heard the whole truth. As their oars dipped into the water, Esther's furious voice wafted towards Tad, in snippets.

' . . . *told* you . . . wasting our time . . . drowned dead . . . '

Mr Jackson answered her, loud and stubborn. 'If you want to give up, and go back to Miss Adah's, you're free to leave. But don't expect me to escort you. That elephant belongs to me, and I'm staying in Cincinnati until I get news of it.'

'*If* you get news of it,' Esther muttered.

'If it's drowned, they'll find the body, sooner or later. If it's not drowned, someone will see it, and tell us. *I won't give up!'*

Of course you won't, Tad thought miserably. He could almost see the heavy, determined jaw and the glaring blue eyes. Relentless. Unavoidable.

The rowboat dipped away and he closed his own eyes and tried to concentrate on Cissie's steady, low whisper.

'. . . hair that ripples like sunset on the water. And soft hands to stroke you calm. To make everything all right again . . . '

But the words wouldn't make a picture for him. The coal smell of Markle was in his nostrils, and Esther's sharp, complaining voice filled his head. Nothing had changed. He was still Tad Hawkins, who blundered and stumbled and failed in everything he did.

Tad Hawkins, who had been wrong ever since the day he was born.

Chapter 18

Esther had taken his voice away. When he went back to croon to Khush, the words came out differently—hesitant and uncertain. He couldn't talk about Ketty and Nebraska with the same easiness as before, because he couldn't believe they were going to get there.

Esther knew what he was really like.

Khush noticed the difference. Instead of eating stolidly, he began to move around, rubbing himself against the boards that held back the coal.

'For heaven's sake!' Cissie said. 'What's the matter with you, Tad? Can't you keep him quiet for a *minute?*' She pushed him out of the way. 'I'll talk. You can clear this place out a bit.'

Khush rumbled a little, but he steadied as Cissie began to talk. Tad took the shovel and the bucket and toiled up and down the ramp. Whenever there was no other boat near, he pulled back the tarpaulin a little further and tipped out a bucketful of filthy straw, into the water.

As he shovelled and tipped, he listened to Cissie's voice, muttering about the wonderful place they were going to, but it didn't mean anything. Nebraska, and Ketty, were as remote as fairytales.

Even Cissie couldn't talk for ever. By the third day, she had almost lost her voice. And Khush had lost his patience.

Instead of eating quietly, he flipped hay around and trampled the straw into a sodden pancake. He rumbled and snorted and complained, and twice he trumpeted loudly, just as steamboats were passing. The heads on the stern decks flicked round to face the coal tow, so quickly that one man lost his hat in the water.

Then, just after midday, the rocking began. Steadily, straining at his tethers, Khush threw his weight first to one side and then to the other, like a child working a swing.

Their barge started to dip and heave, as though it were travelling on the sea. When Tad looked through the gap in the tarpaulins, he could see the other barges responding, straining at the cables which bound them together.

Twice that afternoon, men came from the steamboat to call down to them.

'Cap says you must keep that creature still. Or we'll start losing cargo.'

'Can you not stop him rocking?'

The third time, it was Jedediah himself who came. They heard the crunch of falling coal as he pulled back a tarpaulin and looked down at them.

'I cannot take you any further. Not if it means losing the cargo. I will have to put you ashore.'

He spoke to both of them, but it was Cissie who went scurrying up the ramp to confront him.

'You *promised!* You promised to take me all the way to Cairo!'

Jedediah blinked, but he didn't waver. 'No, sister. I said I would take thee, *God willing*. If thou had been standing with me just now, watching the tow jump about, thou'd know He did not want that creature on board. Not unless it is His purpose to drown us all.'

Cissie pouted. 'What are you going to do with us?'

'There is a landing round that next bend.' Jedediah pointed downstream. 'It is not much used. If thou can keep the creature quiet for half an hour, we will land all three of you there. You can walk the rest of the way to Cairo. It will take no more than a couple of days.'

'A couple of *days?*' Cissie rolled her eyes pathetically and spread her hands, but that didn't make any impression on Jedediah. He had gone already, moving over the surface of the barges as though he were on dry land.

Tad looked up. 'Should we put our things together?'

'I suppose so.' Cissie slid despondently down the ramp,

116

without pulling the tarpaulin back into place. She and Tad began to walk round, taking down the bundles they had hung up, out of the way of Khush's feet.

Khush watched them. Once or twice he unhooked something before Cissie could get it, holding it teasingly above her head. But most of the time he had his trunk raised, breathing in the fresh air from outside.

The coal tow swung round the river bend and then headed out of the channel, towards the right-hand shore. Tad and Cissie had no time to worry or make plans. They were brought up against the bank, with four other coal barges between them and the wooden landing, and Jedediah sang out immediately:

'Passengers ashore!'

Every man on the towboat was staring as Khush climbed out of the dark hole. Jedediah smiled encouragingly.

'You will do all right. When you get to Cairo, ask for Abel Manzoni. Captain of the *Mary Sullivan*. Tell him I sent you.'

'Better take a bath first,' muttered the pilot, from beside Jedediah.

The rest of the crew roared with laughter as Tad and Cissie led Khush on to the shore. Then the great tow swung out left, into the river again.

Khush moved too. He lumbered off downstream, so fast that Tad and Cissie had to leave their bundles and run to keep up with him. He was heading for a place where the bank shelved down into the water. As soon as he reached it, he plunged in, sucking up great trunkfuls of water and squirting them over his back.

Tad looked at him. 'Maybe we should do that, too.'

'Wash? In the *river*?' Cissie stared at him.

She sounded very grand and haughty, like a young lady from the east, with smooth golden ringlets and a fine cloth dress. But she didn't look like that at all.

She was disgusting. Her hair was ragged, her face was dirty and, from thigh to foot, her clothes were caked with straw and dried elephant dung.

'Perhaps you ought to take a look.' Tad waved his hand towards the river in front of them. The water was as smooth as a mirror. 'No one's going to take us on board a steamboat like this.'

Cissie wrinkled her nose. 'You're trying to tell me that I look like—like *you?*'

'I don't know what I—' Tad glanced down. 'I suppose you must.'

'Ugh!' She took one step forwards and flung herself straight into the river.

Tad could have told her that the smooth water was deep. He waited for her to bob up again, but she didn't. Instead, the water began to churn. The hole was deeper than he had guessed.

He kicked off his shoes and dropped into the river. It was easy to find her, because she grabbed hold of his leg and hung on desperately.

'Let go!' Tad panted. 'I can't—'

He slapped her, to force her to loosen her hold, and then towed her down into the shallow water, where Khush was standing.

The moment she was on her feet, she began to scream, slithering and sliding around in the mud.

'I hate you! I hate you! If it weren't for you, we'd still be on the barge! And I wouldn't have fallen into the river! And—'

For a split second, Tad believed her. All his life, people had been saying things like that, and he had been believing them. He opened his mouth to apologize.

And a jet of water hit him square in the face.

Khush had decided to play. The next jet hit Cissie, catching her off balance, so that she staggered and fell over in the water.

'*No, Khush!*' Tad said.

He hauled Cissie to her feet again, and the feel of her thin shoulders brought him to his senses. She wasn't Esther or Aunt Adah. She was younger than he was. And she was cold and tired and suffering from shock.

'You can't hate me,' he said firmly, holding her up. 'I've just saved your life. What you need is something to eat and a good long sleep, and I'm going to make sure that you get that.'

118

He thought she would argue, but she didn't. She flopped against his hands, so suddenly that he almost dropped her.

'That would be good,' she said wearily. 'I'm sorry. I don't know why I—'

Then she broke off, in mid-sentence. Her mouth fell open and she pointed ahead, over Tad's shoulder. He spun round.

A steam tow had come round the bend, on its way up to Cincinnati. And every man on board was hanging over the port rail, staring at Khush.

Yet again, my life has been preserved! This time, it was Tad who saved me. He pulled me out of the river yesterday—when I had thrown myself in, in a desperate attempt to get clean.

I fear—I *hope*—that you would not know me if you saw me now. I am ragged and dirty and (even after my too-enthusiastic bath) *not* well-scented. Now I am settling down to sleep on the ground, beside the Ohio river.

Khush's transgressions caused us to be banished from the coal tow and we have, as it were, been through the Fall of Man in reverse. Having been cast out of Hell, we find ourselves walking through a green Eden, on our way to Cairo. I can almost imagine myself a noble savage. Or that explorer who first travelled the length of this mighty river.

But, even in Eden, hard ground wears out our feet. We walk at night and spend the daylight hours hiding, but that does not save us from blisters. I shall be profoundly grateful when we reach Cairo. I do not think that I can endure much more of this way of travelling.

Tad has studied the maps Mr Nagel gave us, and he says that we should arrive in Cairo tomorrow.

I wish we were there already!

CHAPTER 19

THEY COULDN'T just go on walking. Tad watched Cissie grow tired and pale, and noticed how Khush began to drag his feet. And he hadn't forgotten the men staring from the steam tow. The news about Khush would be up and down the river by now.

They had to have a plan before they marched into Cairo.

Every night he brooded, as they walked slowly along the river bank. He knew he had to talk to Cissie, but he put it off until the last moment. The day before they reached Cairo.

Then he began abruptly, as they settled down to eat before their daylight rest. 'You and Khush should stay here today. We can't go into Cairo together. There may be a trap.'

Cissie glared, and put down her dry bread. 'What happens to me, if you don't come back?'

'I won't be in any danger on my own. I can find Captain Manzoni and come back to get you when the arrangements are made, and Khush can have a rest.'

'A rest?' Cissie looked sulky. 'He's only just started walking. He's been standing still for most of the time since we left Pittsburgh.'

'That's why he's limping.' Tad couldn't believe she hadn't noticed. 'You know how his feet get sore. Look.'

It wasn't easy to show her. But he coaxed and whistled and at last, rumbling crossly, Khush lifted his left back foot. There was a small split by the heel, and when Tad touched it Khush wrenched the foot away and ambled further into the trees.

Tad straightened up. 'He needs a rest. If he keeps it dry and keeps his weight off it, it should heal up.'

'But he can't rest,' Cissie said stubbornly. 'We're going to Nebraska.'

'We shan't lose much time if I go on ahead. It can't be more

121

than twenty miles. I should be able to do that in a day, if I haven't got to worry about hiding Khush. I can travel in the light, while you're sleeping.'

Cissie clenched her fists. 'You're not going off on your own and leaving me here. There's no point in talking about it. I'm coming, and so is Khush.'

She tossed her head and began to eat a dried apple ring.

Tad looked at Khush, who was shuffling round in the wood. Three steps, and then a limp on the fourth. Every time. Tad closed his eyes.

'You have to stay here and give him a rest,' he said quietly. 'If you don't, I'm going back.'

'What?' Cissie gaped.

'If you want him to go lame, I'm not helping you.' Tad opened his eyes again. 'I'll turn straight round and walk back up the river. And I won't stop until I get to Cincinnati.'

He couldn't tell whether Cissie was amazed or furious. She turned bright pink and stared at him, struggling for words. But there was nothing to talk about. Tad walked closer to the river and sat down on the bank to finish his meal.

Cissie let him sit there for ten minutes. He could feel her watching him. Waiting for him to turn round and apologize. But he went on eating steadily, staring across the grey water at the Kentucky shore.

It was Cissie who gave way. She came over and slid on to the bank beside him.

'You mean it?'

Tad shrugged. 'I have to mean it. Can't take a dead elephant to Nebraska.'

'*Dead?*'

'Don't know much about elephants. Only what your pa told me. But he kept on about Khush's skin. *Splits mean infections*, he said. And that heel split's getting worse.'

Cissie hesitated. Tad thought she was going to give him an order, but she didn't. She picked a leaf from the bush beside them and ran it between her fingers. 'I don't think I can bear being left. On my own.'

The hesitation took Tad by surprise. He answered awkwardly, trying hard to be kind. 'You won't be on your own. You'll have Khush.'

'But he's not—' Cissie looked up again. 'You are going to come back? You won't set off and keep going without me?'

Tad blinked. He had been tensing himself for a struggle, but Cissie was avoiding his eyes and staring down at her leaf. 'Of course I'll come back. As soon as I've found Captain Manzoni. Why should I run out on you?'

'Oh, I don't know.' Cissie began to pull the leaf to pieces. 'You might be tired of being ordered about. You might not think much of me—'

Tad looked sideways at her. He could not see her face, but he saw the jagged fragments of leaf falling from her hands.

'You'll be fine,' he said gently. 'Staying here—that's nothing. Not after all you've done.'

'I'm not good at keeping still,' she muttered. 'Nor at waiting with nothing to do.'

She dropped the rest of the leaf all at once, in a shower of green tatters, and clenched her hands. Her fists looked very small.

But Tad knew he mustn't give way. 'You'll be fine,' he said again. 'Just stay here with Khush. And be ready to go when I get back from Cairo.'

'But—'

Cissie lifted her head, and he saw her lip tremble. He reached out a hand towards her and tweaked her ear, very gently.

'I shan't be long.'

Then he jumped to his feet, pulled a piece of bread out of the food bag and set off for Cairo.

It was further than he expected. When he reached Mound City, and saw the boats lined up beside the river, he was sure he had arrived in Cairo. For half an hour, he asked after Captain Manzoni, until someone told him he was in the wrong city.

First mistake, he thought wryly, as he set off again, to walk

123

the last few miles. He hoped there wouldn't be a second.

But he made the second one almost as soon as he reached Cairo.

He came in from the north-east, and he knew, from Mr Nagel's map, that the city was a triangle, built on the land between the Ohio and the Mississippi. He should have headed straight through the triangle, to find the wharf where the Mississippi steamboats tied up.

But it was almost dark. Cairo sat on low ground, surrounded by high levees to hold the water back. Once Tad was in the streets, he couldn't see either river, and it was easy to forget that he was in a river town at all. There was no one about, to direct him to the wharf. The stores were empty, and no men stood chatting on street corners.

But from the first hotel he saw came a blaze of light, throwing a yellow stripe diagonally across his path.

It was the light that led him astray. His feet were aching and his legs were tired. The light from the hotel meant warmth and rest and a place to sit down while he asked his questions. He wavered for a moment and then turned out of his way and walked up to the hotel door.

At that moment, someone began to come out, pushing the door open from inside.

Even then, everything might have been all right, if Tad had had the sense to keep out of sight. If he had stepped back into the shadows, his face would have been invisible.

But, as the door opened, he realized that it was a woman coming out. Aunt Adah had always insisted that he should open doors politely for women, from the moment he could walk. Now he did it automatically, standing in the diagonal stripe of light to hold the door out of the way.

The woman swished through, walking briskly. She didn't thank Tad, but as she turned left, up the street, she couldn't avoid seeing his face. And when she did, her eyes opened wide.

They recognized each other at the same instant, but she reacted first. Before Tad could blink, she grabbed his sleeve and snapped, 'Don't you dare move, Thaddeus Hawkins!'

For a second, he froze. Her voice, and her cold eyes, and the grip of her sharp fingers, mesmerized him by their hateful familiarity. He obeyed her, out of sheer habit.

CHAPTER 20

HE WAS only still for a second. But that gave Esther time to fasten her fingers firmly, and she didn't let go.

Dragging backwards, Tad caught his foot in a broom that was propped against the front wall of the hotel. He staggered sideways and knocked over a bucket beside the broom. Dirty water swilled round the bottom of Esther's skirt.

'You haven't changed, have you?' She looked down in disgust at her wet hem, but she didn't move. And she certainly didn't loosen her grip. Digging her fingers into his shoulder, she called back into the hotel.

'Hannibal! Just look who's here!'

Tad wrenched himself backwards, making a last effort to get free, but it was no use. Mr Jackson was already coming through the door. He caught hold of Tad's other arm.

'Now!' he said, very softly.

Esther patted Tad's cheek, catching it with her nails. 'I don't think he's too anxious to stay with us,' she murmured. 'Maybe we should go somewhere quieter.'

Mr Jackson nodded, and his eyes swivelled towards the alley at the side of the hotel. 'We'll take him up to the room. Round the back way.'

'And don't you dare to make a noise!' Esther hissed in Tad's ear. 'Or I'll swear you tried to pick my pocket.'

Numbly, he let them haul him down the side of the hotel and in at the back door. No one saw them climb the stairs or open the door of the shabby back bedroom, and none of them said a word.

But the moment the bedroom door was shut, Mr Jackson threw Tad straight across the room, so that he landed on the bed, bruising his hip on the medicine bottle in his pocket. He lay there, looking up at Mr Jackson. Taking in the solid, muscular strength of that heavy body.

126

Mr Jackson let him look, smiling slightly, as though he knew what Tad was thinking. Then he came forward and leaned over the bed.

'Where's my elephant?'

There was no threat. No need for a threat. That thick, harsh voice was enough on its own. Tad shuddered and looked away. But that only showed him Esther, standing with her back against the door and her arms folded and her thin lips pressed together.

'There's no way out.' Mr Jackson jabbed a finger into Tad's chest. 'You're going to tell us.'

Not a word, Tad thought, desperately. They were both watching everything he did, every move he made. If he started talking, he was sure to make a mistake. He would say something about Khush, or about Cissie, that would give away where they were. He had to stay utterly silent.

He lay without moving, gazing up stubbornly.

'Do you want me to bring the law into it?' Mr Jackson said, jabbing again.

Tad thought about being in jail. But he didn't say anything. Even the law couldn't *make* him talk. And he could see Esther thinking the same thing. She gave her head a quick, impatient little shake, setting her curls swinging.

'Or there's a quicker way . . . ' Mr Jackson's hand slid threateningly inside his jacket.

Tad had seen the little shoulder-holster, hanging on the back of the bedroom door at Aunt Adah's. He knew what the gun was like. He lay very still, and watched Mr Jackson's hand move, under the cloth.

But Esther's head gave another little shake. 'Maybe we don't need that either. Let me talk to him a while.'

For a moment, Mr Jackson looked startled, as though he had not expected her to speak. Then his hand slid out of the jacket, empty, and he sat down on the broken cane chair by the window.

Esther looked across the room at Tad, and her eyes glittered. 'I never thought you'd get this far. You've come a thousand miles from home, and you're still in one piece.'

She was getting ready to be cruel. Tad knew that look, that false note of gaiety. He curled his hands into fists and waited.

'But where are you going now?' Esther smiled, showing the points of her teeth. 'You can't go on travelling west. Not with an *elephant.*'

She paused, looking him up and down, and Tad struggled to keep his face blank. He didn't want to give away anything about where they were going. But he felt as though *Nebraska* were written on his forehead.

'You'll never manage, west of the Mississippi,' Esther murmured.

Her words wriggled into his ears and seeped to the back of his brain. She hadn't forgotten how to make him feel he was wrong. *Never put the pan lids in that cupboard . . . rub the marble again, with a dry cloth . . . go back to the store, and make them give you full weight . . .*

Tad pressed his lips together. He didn't know what she was up to, but he knew that he mustn't speak.

Esther smirked. 'Have you never heard of the Great American Desert? That's where you'll get, if you go on travelling west. In winter, the snow is deep enough to cover a man's head. In summer, the water dries up and the sun shrivels all the plants. And in between, there are plagues of grasshoppers, that eat every blade of green . . . '

Don't listen. Tad tried to conjure up his picture of the wide, grassy prairie. Of the frame house, and the shady garden, and the smiling woman on the porch.

But the green faded away before he could fix it in his mind. The shady trees shrivelled and the figure on the porch had Esther's mocking face. Esther's harsh, dream-shattering voice.

'That elephant will die of cold in the winter, if you take it west. Unless it dies of hunger and thirst, before that.'

Tad shook his head from side to side, to clear out her words. Esther smiled.

'You know where they are, don't you? It would be better if you told us.' Her hand, in its pale, smooth glove, ran up and down the shabby door. The glove was a delicate fawn colour, with a long smear of dirt running down one finger. 'Cissie

Keenan is hardly more than a child. She'll lead you into trouble, if you let her.'

Don't listen, Tad told himself. *They don't know anything, and they can't force you to tell.*

Esther's eyes grew sharper. 'But Cissie *isn't* a child. Is she? She's older than that. Too old to be travelling round with a boy like you, on her own.'

Slowly and deliberately, she let her eyes move across the room, until she was staring at the dressing-table. At her own silver-backed hairbrush, lying there beside Mr Jackson's comb. Her long, bent hairpins, scattered over one of his handkerchiefs.

Tad turned a hot, angry red and clenched his fists.

Esther let her eyes linger for a moment on his face. Then she stepped away from the door. 'You need time to think things over, Tad. Then you'll remember how young you are. How—prone to disasters.' She slid her arm through Mr Jackson's and looked up at him. 'Shall we go for a walk, and leave Tad to come to his senses?'

Mr Jackson stared down at her for a second, raising his eyebrows. She pulled his arm.

'I *know* Tad,' she said softly.

A small, unpleasant smile slid over Mr Jackson's face. He glanced once at Tad and then escorted Esther out of the room, closing the door behind them and turning the key in the lock.

Tad sat up and put his head in his hands. Bits of what Esther had said swirled round in his brain like evil spells. *Prone to disasters . . . too old to be travelling round with a boy like you . . . the Great American Desert . . .*

And there was the gun. And the shadow of the law. And Mr Jackson's cold, brutal eyes.

. . . prone to disasters . . .

He tried to drag his thoughts together, but he was still the boy from Miss Adah's house. The blundering, clumsy fool, with a weight on his conscience that could never be lifted. The more Esther battered away at him, the more foolish and stupid he would feel. And *wrong*. He had to get away, before she persuaded him that he couldn't trust his own judgement.

He had to escape.

I am left here with Khush, while Tad goes ahead to Cairo—and I cannot bear it!

How did you change your life so easily, Ketty? When you were Kerstin Gilstring, you moved constantly, from town to town and from one excitement to another. How can you tolerate being plain Fru Svensson, sweeping an earth floor in Nebraska?

How can you endure all those empty hours? With nothing but the thoughts inside your head?

Since the crash, I find it a sort of torture to be on my own. Tad is so large and steady that he makes a wall between me and my thoughts. But when he is not here, they torment me worse than the mosquitoes.

And I am shut in with them, closed off from the real business of life. I need to be outside, where things are done and decided.

I need the seat by the window . . .

I must go on! I have tried, but I *cannot* stay here any longer. Better to quarrel with Tad than to sit here alone with my thoughts. I shall take Khush and head for Cairo, as soon as it is dark.

CHAPTER 21

THE WINDOW was small and barred. The door was locked. Tad spent ten minutes looking helplessly from one to the other, sure that there was no way to escape.

But he had to get out. Opening the window, he ran his fingers over every inch of the bars, looking for a weak place, or a fixing that he could loosen. But the bars were strong and straight, and set deep into the brickwork.

Maybe the door.

He rattled the handle and pulled at it, but nothing moved. The lock was solid. Angrily, he slumped sideways against the door, letting it take his weight.

It shuddered. And, from outside in the corridor, came a faint noise. A high, metallic chink on the oilcloth.

The sound of the key falling out of the lock.

Tad threw himself to the ground and peered under the door. There it was. A big, grey key, lying only an inch or so away from him. He couldn't get his fingers under the door, but there must be something in the room that he could use. There *had* to be.

There was! And Esther herself had shown it to him! He leaped up and raced to the dressing-table. There were five of the long, brown hairpins, and he snatched up three of them.

It took less than a minute. Twisting the hairpins together, he made a long, strong hook that slid easily under the door. After a little scrabbling, he managed to slide the hook through the loop at the top of the key and pull it back into the room.

He could hardly believe that Esther had been so stupid, but he didn't stand around wondering. Quickly, he pushed the key into the lock and opened the door. Then, slowly and carefully, he slipped out of the room and began to creep along the corridor.

It was impossible to move without making a noise. The floorboards creaked, the stairs squeaked, and the back door, when he reached it, squealed loudly on its hinges. But miraculously—unbelievably—no one came.

The street was almost completely dark. Tad stood for a moment, hesitating. He could run down to the wharf and look for Captain Manzoni, but that would make it easy to pick up his trail.

Better to go back to Cissie. Maybe they ought to change their plans completely, now Mr Jackson had tracked them down. He needed to talk to her.

Quietly, keeping close to the buildings at the side of the road, he walked up the street and out of Cairo. He was tired now, and every time he heard a footstep, his pulse jumped, but he didn't dare look round. He made himself stroll slowly, not attracting anyone's attention.

Once he was out of the town, he took the plain, well-worn track by the river, half-running at first and then settling to a steady walk. There was a shred of moon, but it was hard to see his way and he needed to keep to the path.

At first, he stopped whenever there was a noise from behind. There seemed to be far more sounds than when he was going into Cairo. Sticks cracked, leaves rustled and branches swished. But whenever he looked back, all he could see was senseless, tangled shadows.

In the end, he decided that they were the ordinary noises of the night, magnified by his nervousness. It would be better to ignore them, and go as fast as he could.

It wouldn't be long before Esther and Mr Jackson went back to the room, and the moment they did, they would be out looking for him. He couldn't afford to hang around peering at shadows.

He walked steadily, without seeing anyone, until he got back to Mound City. But there the darkness was full of people. A quarrel had spilled out of the hotel and the crowds in the street were shouting threats at each other. For a moment, Tad hesitated on the edge of the town.

Then he remembered that he was alone. With Khush, he

would have had to walk round the outside of the town, to avoid being noticed. But he was just an ordinary boy now, with nothing to draw attention to him. It would be much better to go straight through, and not risk losing the trail he was following.

He slipped quietly down one side of the street, slid past the crowds, and was out of town again in a few moments. Then he went on walking automatically, putting his tired feet one in front of the other. He wasn't sure how far it was to the little wood where he had left Cissie and Khush, but he was impatient to see it. They had to move straight away, in case anyone had caught sight of them.

By the time he reached the wood, the sky was beginning to brighten, very faintly. Four o'clock in the morning, or maybe five. Still too early for many birds to sing, but light enough for him to make out Khush's huge, black shape.

He peered ahead, straining his eyes. He wanted to see that shape. To walk up to Khush and rest his head on the broad, smooth side that could take his whole weight without faltering.

But Khush didn't appear.

He still hadn't appeared by the time Tad reached the middle of the wood. Maybe he was lying down.

Ten yards further on, Tad knew there was no elephant in the scrubby patch of trees. No girl, either. Nothing but a square of trampled bushes and a single leaf of paper, fluttering on a branch.

He tugged the paper down and peered, but it was still too dark. Even when he carried it out into the open, away from the trees, there wasn't enough light to read the words.

If only he had a lantern—

As if in answer to his wish, a match flared. For a second, Tad saw the small, neat letters.

If you read this, something has gone wrong, because I should have met you at the Mary Sullivan. *I will wait there for you.*

Do not be angry—C

Then Mr Jackson pulled the paper out of his hand.

133

'So near,' he said, 'and yet so far.' He stared at the message for a moment and then crumpled the paper and threw it to the ground.

Tad closed his eyes. 'You meant to leave that key in the door,' he said slowly. 'You wanted me to get out and lead you here.'

'It was Esther's idea.' Mr Jackson smiled, drily. 'That girl has more brains than I gave her credit for, but she couldn't keep up with you. I had to leave her half-way. In Mound City.'

Mound City! Tad's mind raced. *That* was where he had missed Cissie and Khush! Cissie wouldn't have taken him through the town. Not with all those people about. She had gone round the back, keeping clear of the houses. And now she would be almost in Cairo.

Mr Jackson seized his arm, pushing it up, viciously, behind his back. 'Let's get going, then. It's a long walk back to Cairo.'

'But—'

Tad's legs ached almost past bearing. He was exhausted, and he knew Mr Jackson could see it. But there was no escape.

Mr Jackson gave another agonizing twist to his arm. 'I know where the *Mary Sullivan* is moored. I saw her yesterday. We must try to get back there before she sails.'

For a second, the little gun appeared in front of Tad's face, as a reminder. Then Mr Jackson gave him a hard push, and the two of them were on their way.

It seemed impossible. Tad was hungry and tired, and he had already walked more than twenty miles. But Mr Jackson dragged and prodded and shouted, and somehow his feet kept moving.

When they reached Mound City, it was clear daylight, and Esther was waiting for them. Mr Jackson hired a couple of horses and Tad finished the journey behind Esther, trying not to fall asleep.

As they rattled into Cairo, he and Esther were left behind. Mr Jackson trotted ahead, making straight for the wharf, and by the time they caught him up, he had already dismounted. He was talking to an old man sitting on a bollard.

'You've missed her, all right,' the old man said, with relish. 'You don't get a sight like that every day. Everyone in Cairo was down here to cheer. A great elephant! Stuck up on the deck!'

He shook his head admiringly and waved a hand at the long plume of smoke that floated high above the distant trees.

'There she goes. The *Mary Sullivan*. With an elephant on board.'

He spat a long stream of tobacco juice at Mr Jackson's feet and nodded to himself.

'Seen a lot of things going up the Mississip, but I never thought to see that. A mighty great *elephant*.'

CHAPTER 22

'YOU LITTLE demon!' Esther slid out of the saddle and pulled Tad after her. 'It was a plot, wasn't it? That girl sent you into Cairo first, to keep us out of the way!'

'No!' Tad stumbled against the horse and it jittered sideways, sending him staggering. 'I thought—she was supposed to stay in the wood and wait for me—'

But she hadn't. She'd gone and left him behind. He stared at the column of smoke rising beyond the housetops and wondered what to do next.

Esther began to shake him, hissing furiously. '*She* planned it, didn't she? *You're* too stupid to think of something like that! But you do whatever she tells you to—'

'No!'

The other people on the wharf were beginning to stare at them. Mr Jackson came across and put a finger on Esther's arm.

'Don't shake his brains out. We might need him.'

Esther snorted. 'What brains?'

But she let go and stepped back, straightening her battered bonnet. Mr Jackson smiled nastily at Tad.

'Well, she's tricked you, the same as she tricked me. Gone off with the elephant, and left you behind. She's a cheap little cheat, just like her father.'

Tad looked away. Michael Keenan. Cissie. For a second, their pictures blurred and twisted into ugliness inside his head.

Esther was watching him. When she spoke again, her voice was very soft. 'Wouldn't you like to get your own back, Tad? It's very easy. You just have to tell us where she's going.'

The words seeped into Tad's mind. Slow and soft, like a slug crawling up a wall.

'Is she heading for St Louis?' Esther asked, coaxingly. 'If she is, we can get there before her. We only have to take the railroad. Then we can catch her, and you can get your own back.'

Get your own back. Twice she had used the same slug-words, and they sickened Tad. He looked at the vanishing smoke of the steamboat, and thought of Khush.

Mr Jackson put a thick hand on Tad's shoulder. 'I'll make it worth your while. Just tell me where she's taking my elephant.'

My elephant. But Mr Jackson had scrubbed at Khush's side like someone scouring a block of stone. Tad remembered how Khush had rumbled and snatched the broom away.

'How about it?' Mr Jackson was watching him. 'You can have your railroad fare home, if that's what you want.'

'I—'

Tad pretended to sulk. But while he dragged his feet through the dust, his brain was whirring. Cissie would be going straight to St Louis. To look for a boat going up the Missouri. If Mr Jackson took the railroad, he would be there to catch her, before she arrived. But if he went on a boat, following her . . .

'Oh, leave the fool!' Esther said. 'He doesn't know anything. He's too stupid.'

'I don't know exactly,' Tad muttered, still looking down at his feet. 'But I've got a kind of idea—'

Mr Jackson pulled a handful of coins out of his pocket and held them under Tad's nose. 'Let's hear your idea.'

Tad lowered his voice to a dramatic whisper. 'She said it was up the Mississippi.'

Mr Jackson's fingers half-closed round the coins. 'What was up the Mississippi?'

'Her aunt's. Where she's going. *We'll see Aunt Eliza before we hit St Louis.* That's what she used to say. I was going to get a job there.'

Tad glanced up, and saw two pairs of suspicious eyes watching him. He grabbed Mr Jackson's sleeve.

'I don't know what to do now. Take me with you! Please!'

'Take *you?*' Esther said scornfully. 'You're no use to anyone. Let go of Mr Jackson's coat. You're crumpling it.'

Tad gripped the coat even tighter and looked up, as desperately as he could. 'Please!'

For one unnerving moment, it seemed as though Mr Jackson might agree. 'The boy might be useful,' he said thoughtfully.

'Rubbish!' Esther flicked her gloved hand at Tad's arm, knocking it away. 'We don't want to waste time on him. We have to find a boat to take us up the Mississippi.'

'It's a long river,' Mr Jackson said drily.

'We'll just have to ask at every landing, all the way up.' Esther tossed her head. 'People are sure to notice if the elephant's on board. We'll catch it in the end.'

Tad stood between the two of them while they argued round him.

Go on, he was thinking. *Get on your steamboat and stop at every landing.* If they did that, they would never catch the *Mary Sullivan* before it reached St Louis. Cissie could keep ahead, as long as she caught the first Missouri steamboat she could.

But how would she know she had to do that?

She needed to know that she was being chased. Otherwise, she might spend too long hanging around in St Louis.

He had to get there first, and warn her.

Tad looked at Esther and Mr Jackson. They weren't taking any notice of him, but they would be suspicious if he slipped away. He needed an excuse.

Whirling round, he seized the sleeve of Esther's dress and wailed plaintively at her. 'Please, Esther, don't leave me here on my own! I can't manage! I don't know what to do! I'm frightened—'

For a moment, he thought he had ruined it, by sounding too spineless. But Esther believed it all. She snatched the coins from Mr Jackson's hand and dropped them into Tad's pocket. Then she pushed him backwards, screeching angrily.

'Go away! Just go away! If I have to watch you hanging around any longer, I'll be SICK! Get out of here!'

Mr Jackson whispered something in her ear, and some of the women standing round muttered disapprovingly, but Tad took the chance she had offered. Despondently, dragging his feet, he sidled away from the river.

It took all his self-control to keep moving slowly until he was out of sight, but he managed it. And it worked. Before he disappeared round the nearest corner, Esther and Mr Jackson lost interest in him. He saw them turn away and begin to ask about boats to St Louis.

Grinning to himself, Tad rounded the corner and began to run, weaving his way through the streets of Cairo. When he was a safe distance from the river, he slowed to a trot and watched for someone in a hurry.

It didn't take long. A woman with four little children came bustling out of a house in front of him. Tad stepped up to her.

'Please, ma'am, could you direct me to the railroad depot?'

She didn't even look up at him. 'Which one would that be?'

'I want to go to St Louis.'

She waved a hand. 'Up there, turn left and then follow the tracks.'

By that time, her children were away and round the next corner, and she scurried off without having seen Tad at all. He grinned again. *She* wouldn't be telling anyone where he had gone.

Five minutes later, he was walking into the depot. The ticket clerk was reading a newspaper and he barely glanced up. 'Yes?'

Tad put his hand into his pocket and pulled out Mr Jackson's money. 'I want to go to St Louis, please.'

I have lost Tad.

I cannot understand how it happened. There is nowhere to get lost in Cairo. It is nothing but a poor, swampy triangle of land, where the Ohio joins the Mississippi. Sitting on that triangle, Cairo is bounded by rivers on two sides and walled in by defences against the water.

I thought I was safe to take Khush on board this boat. Everyone in Cairo knew where I was, and it seemed certain that Tad would find me. But he never came.

He set out to enquire for Captain Manzoni, and for his ship, the *Mary Sullivan*. And that was an easy task. I accomplished it myself within fifteen minutes of reaching Cairo.

I arrived before dawn, but immediately seven people appeared, to inspect Khush. Within ten minutes, the seven had become thirty, and they conducted me to the *Mary Sullivan* out of sheer, helpful curiosity. I found Captain Manzoni just roused from his bunk and half-way through shaving.

Since I had found him, it seemed only sensible to tell him why I had come. And within twenty minutes we had struck the kind of deal that Pa used to make.

I went on board the *Mary Sullivan* while she was moored, showing off Khush to interested parties at fifty cents a head (the proceeds to be split with the good captain). And I persuaded six passengers to travel today instead of tomorrow, so that they might ever afterwards bore their friends and family with *How I Went up the Mississippi with an Elephant*. (In consequence of which, our fares are halved.)

I never thought that I was running myself into a trap for I was sure that Tad would discover where I was. The whole of *Cairo* knew where I was! But Tad did not come. And the captain wanted to set out.

The boat was advertised to start at nine in the morning. By ten, I could delay it no longer. Nor could I go ashore. I had made my bargain with Captain Manzoni, and he would not let me break it.

We left at five past ten. I stared over the stern rail until Cairo went out of sight, hoping that Tad would run on to the wharf, red-faced and panting, with that apologetic smile he has, (which could so easily trick you into thinking him foolish).

But he did not come.

So I am on my own. An object of the most *acute* curiosity to everyone on the boat. Elegant ladies take me for a poor heathen boy and press tracts into my hand. Gamblers surround Khush, making bets about his every movement. There is a scientific gentleman who plagues me with elephantine questions (some of them so direct that he would *expire* if he knew I was female). And a lady of artistic temperament who is so eager to 'draw this mighty creature from life' that she has set up her easel in the way of everyone else.

I hope Tad will follow me to St Louis. I do not know why he should, for he must surely think I have deserted him. But he is not easily turned aside. I pray that, having set out for Nebraska, he will remain determined to reach it.

He *must* come!

CHAPTER 23

THE TRAIN broke down when it reached Marys River.

Tad had been asleep, curled in a corner of the seat, and when he woke up he was confused. He thought for a moment that they had reached St Louis.

But the woman over the aisle soon put him right. 'We won't get there tonight. They've unhitched the engine and taken it away.'

She was a thin bony woman, not very young, in a worn, brown coat. Her dull hair was twisted into tight, unlikely ringlets and she sat stiffly, clutching her bag.

'Taken the *engine* away?' Tad felt his stomach turn over. 'But I've got to get to St Louis.'

'We've all got to get to St Louis,' the woman said. An odd smile twitched at her mouth. 'But we'll have to wait until tomorrow.'

'But—'

If he couldn't get to St Louis before Mr Jackson and Esther, his plan was ruined. He swallowed and gritted his teeth.

The woman peered across the aisle at him. Then she wrenched her bag open and pulled out a small parcel. 'Looks as though you could do with this.'

Tad hesitated, staring stupidly, and she shook the parcel.

'Come on! Take it!'

He stumbled over to sit next to her and she dropped it into his lap. A flat, damp bundle, wrapped in a cloth. When he peeled the cloth away, there was a thick slice of pecan pie inside. After days of dry bread and cheese, the smell of the pie was almost too much to bear. Tad swallowed again.

'But— isn't this your supper, ma'am?'

She shook her head, and the ringlets jerked and swung. 'Can't seem to fancy it. You can have it.'

'I—thank you.'

He couldn't go on talking. Not with the pie there. He bit into it, closing his eyes.

When he opened them again, the woman was studying his torn clothes and his splitting boots.

'Looks like you can't afford to eat. How come you had the money for this train?'

'I—I—' Tad had a mouth full of pecan pie and a blank mind. He struggled to think of a story that would satisfy the woman. But before he could say anything she snapped her bag shut and her thin face turned a dull red.

'Don't take any notice of me. Nosy old maid. Got nothing better to do than mind other people's business.'

'It's all right,' Tad said awkwardly. 'If you want to know—'

Her face burned even redder. 'Didn't mean to pry. Just wanted to know if you were all right. You seemed in a rare hurry to get to St Louis.'

'I'm supposed to be meeting someone,' Tad mumbled. 'We're going west.'

'Going west?' The woman fidgeted with the catch of her bag. 'Where are you headed?'

'Nebraska, ma'am.'

'Nebraska . . . '

She sat and watched him eating the pie. Looking away uneasily, Tad found himself gazing at her hands. They were twisted tightly together on top of her bag. As he finished the last piece of pie, they clenched even harder, until the knuckles whitened.

'What part of Nebraska would that be?' she said.

'It's—' Tad hesitated. But it couldn't do any harm to tell her. 'The Looking Glass Creek country, ma'am.'

'Looking Glass Creek.' Her voice shook slightly. 'Where exactly would that be?'

'I—' He didn't know. Not exactly. 'I have to get a steamboat at St Louis. To go up the Missouri.'

The woman half closed her eyes. Staring down at her clenched hands, Tad saw them twist. 'I'm taking a steamboat up the Missouri myself,' she said stiffly. 'Maybe we could keep each other company?'

143

'You're going to Nebraska?' Tad couldn't keep the surprise out of his voice. She wasn't his idea of a pioneer.

'I—' With a quick, compulsive movement, the woman dug into her bag and pulled out an envelope. 'Here!' she said fiercely. 'Read that. You might as well know.'

Awkwardly, Tad pulled the folded letter out of the envelope and spread it on his knee. It was very short, written in a cramped, unpractised hand.

Dear Miss Whitwell,
I got your letter, about my advertisement. I wanted someone younger, but 31 is not too bad so long as you're in good health. Maybe we shall suit. The only way to find out is to give it a try. If you want to come, write and tell me when and I will meet you at Omaha.
Yours respectfully,
William Ellicott.

Tad didn't understand. 'You've got a job?'

'You could call it that,' Miss Whitwell said. She looked him straight in the eye. 'I'm going to marry Mr Ellicott.'

'Marry him?' Tad stared. 'He was advertising for a *wife?*'

'Ridiculous, isn't it?' Miss Whitwell gave a quick, bitter bark of laughter. 'Going off to marry a complete stranger. At my age.'

Tad looked down at the hands clenched on her lap and didn't know what to say.

'Ever hear a more foolish reason for going west?' Her voice was brittle and her cheeks had turned a high, hectic red. 'I haven't dared tell a soul. Only you.'

'Me?' Tad looked up at her flushed face, and the way her eyes avoided his, and he understood.

She had no one else. No one who wouldn't laugh and make fun of her and gossip. She needed someone to tell her she wasn't being foolish, but the only person she dared to ask was a ragged stranger on a train.

Tad looked down at the empty pie cloth in his lap.

'There are lots of crazier reasons for going west,' he said slowly. 'Take me. I'm chasing an elephant.'

'An *elephant*?' Miss Whitwell twitched the pie cloth off his lap and began to fold it up. But she was listening.

'If I don't get to St Louis before tomorrow, the elephant will probably get caught, and then it will all have been for nothing—'

Tad's voice started to shake. He stopped for a second, to get it back under control, and Miss Whitwell grinned at him.

'Looks like we've both got troubles. I've told you mine. It's your turn now.'

'I—'

'It'll make you feel better. And who knows—I might be able to help.'

He didn't believe that. But he knew she wouldn't laugh. And she wouldn't give him away, either. All at once, it seemed the only sensible thing to do. He took a deep breath and began.

CHAPTER 24

'So THIS is the magic tincture?' Miss Whitwell held Tad's little bottle high in the air, tilting it so that the clouded green liquid caught the light.

'The only bottle that's left, ma'am.'

'And the elephant lifted her right up in the air?'

Tad nodded. 'Above our heads. And she just lay there in his trunk, as if she'd fainted.'

Little, frail Cissie. Looking as though she couldn't do a thing for herself. With her head flopped sideways and her skirt rucked up.

'Criminal,' Miss Whitwell said severely. 'Cheating honest folk out of their dollars.' She grinned her unexpected, schoolboy grin. 'But I reckon they had their money's worth. It's not every day you get to see a show like that.'

She had made Tad tell her everything, from the moment he first saw Cissie, and she had listened avidly, drinking in all the details and asking lots of sharp, complicated questions. There had been no apologies for prying, either.

Now she stared into the green depths of the liquid, almost dreamily. 'I'd be glad of the chance to see that elephant.'

'So would I,' Tad said. He wondered when they would get to St Louis, and whether Khush would still be there.

Miss Whitwell sniffed. 'I should trust that girl, if I were you. She sounds as though she's got her wits about her. She won't hang around in St Louis.'

That didn't make Tad feel any better. 'You mean she'll go on up the Missouri? Without waiting for me?'

'If she's got any sense she will. No point in sitting about waiting to be caught. She'll be looking for another boat, the moment she gets there.'

'But I don't know where she's going.'

'I said you should trust her!' Miss Whitwell tapped him

sharply on the knee. 'She won't lose you. Not if she's the girl I take her for. She'll know how much she needs you.'

'Needs me?' Tad nearly laughed out loud.

Miss Whitwell nodded, firmly. 'You wait and see. When we get to St Louis.'

The moment the train arrived, she grabbed Tad's arm and marched him out of the depot.

'Got to get on to the wharf. Find out what's happened.'

She walked very fast, with a long, strong stride, and she knew exactly how to find out what she wanted. As soon as they reached the wharf, she began to peer round.

'Waste of time talking to all these men. We need a sensible boy. Around your age. Boys wriggle their noses into everything.' Marching up to the first likely-looking boy, she barked out her question. When she spoke the word *elephant*, his face glowed.

'I should think I *have* seen an elephant! They put him aboard the *Sarah Dewar* first thing this morning. And you shoulda seen 'em load him in. Went straight up the stage plank like a Christian, and on to the boiler deck. They packed him round with bales and boxes till there warn't nothing to be seen but the tip of his trunk.'

Tad couldn't wait to hear all that. 'And is the boat still here?'

'Still here?' The boy stared at him. 'What would she still be here for? That's not much of a way to win a bet!'

'A bet?' Miss Whitwell glanced at Tad. 'What bet would that be?'

The boy grinned, annoyingly. 'The bet on the race.'

What race? Tad would have asked that, but Miss Whitwell put her hand over his mouth and looked severely at the boy. 'If you're aiming to tell us, we'll listen. But we haven't got time to play games.'

'You're mighty interested in that elephant.' The boy stared curiously at her. 'Have you got anything to do with the people chasing it? The ones who telegraphed from Cairo?'

147

Of course, Mr Jackson would have telegraphed! He should have guessed! Tad groaned, but couldn't say anything, because Miss Whitwell's hand was still pressed over his mouth.

'Maybe we have,' she said calmly. 'Is everything ready for them?'

'Sure is, ma'am.' The boy's eyes glittered. 'There's half of St Louis backing them to catch the elephant. And the *City of Omaha*'s ready to take them, the moment they get here. Her captain stands to win five hundred dollars if she catches the *Sarah Dewar*.'

Tad ducked away from Miss Whitwell's hand. 'But the *Sarah Dewar*'s got a start. Hasn't she?'

'Won't be more than four hours.' The boy gave him a pitying look. 'She's nothing but an old tub—and she's got an elephant on board, to slow her down. My money's on the *Omaha*.'

'But—'

Tad wanted to ask more questions, but Miss Whitwell was already dragging him away.

'Got to get ourselves on the *City of Omaha*,' she muttered into his ear. 'Sounds like Jackson will be on that.'

'But ma'am—' Tad pulled his arm free. 'I can't.'

'*Can't?* Why ever not?'

'I can't buy a ticket. I haven't got enough money.'

Miss Whitwell shook her head at him, setting her ridiculous ringlets swinging.

'Fiddle! I'll buy your ticket.'

Her face was flushed with excitement. Not the dull, uncomfortable red she had turned on the train, but a lively crimson.

'I can't let you pay for me,' Tad said awkwardly.

'Why not? You think I should keep my money for Mr Ellicott?'

'I—'

She rapped him smartly on the nose with one finger. 'Don't teach me my business! You stand here and watch for Jackson and that woman of his. I'll see to the tickets.'

148

She was off, before Tad could catch his breath. He walked up and down, expecting at every moment to hear Mr Jackson's bellow or see a purple feather waving down the wharf. They were sure to see him, and catch him again.

But they didn't come. And when Miss Whitwell got back, she was triumphant. She had their tickets in one hand, and she was waving a little white envelope in the other.

'I *told* you that girl wouldn't lose you!'

Tad stared at the envelope. There was his name on the front, written in Cissie's small, scratchy writing. 'Where did you get it?'

'Simple!' Miss Whitwell looked smug. 'She left it in the office, of course. Where I went to book the tickets for the *Omaha*. I just walked in and said, *Any messages for Mr Tad Hawkins?*' She shook the envelope impatiently. 'Go on! See what she says!'

Tad slid his finger under the flap and ripped it up. Inside the envelope was one small piece of paper. With four words on it.

Watch for the ribbons

Miss Whitwell read it over his shoulder. 'What ribbons?'

Tad blinked.

'Come on, boy. What does she mean?'

'She didn't have any ribbons,' Tad said slowly. 'Only—'

Only the ribbons in her drawers. Hanging above his head, bright scarlet, when Khush lifted her into the air. Flashing shamelessly in front of him, in Mr Nagel's barn. But he couldn't mention those. Not to a lady like Miss Whitwell.

He turned away. 'Don't know what she's talking about.'

'Hmm.' Miss Whitwell looked hard at him, but she didn't ask any more questions. She began to walk along the wharf, hunting for the *City of Omaha*.

'We want to find it, and get on board,' she said. 'Jackson's coming up on a boat called the *Katydid*, and there's dozens of people ready to rush him over here, the moment he gets in. Sounds like the whole town's been betting on this race.'

The *City of Omaha* was almost the last steamboat in the

long, elegant queue along the waterfront. A big, new boat, with her brass gleaming and an army of black stokers sweating round her furnaces. Miss Whitwell looked approvingly at the boiler deck.

'That's the place for you. Don't want them spotting you. And if that Esther woman's anything like you've described her, she won't come anywhere near the engines.'

She hauled Tad on board and found a space for him near the boilers. A warm corner, hidden between two heaps of boxes. It was just the sort of place a boy might choose to shelter in, where he could see and not be noticed.

'You should be safe enough here.'

Tad looked up at her. Her ringlets were limp and drooping, but her whole face had come alive. 'It's very kind of you, ma'am.'

'Nonsense! I'm enjoying myself! Just you tell me when those two elephant-chasers come aboard. I want to be sure and recognize them.'

It was another half an hour before the *Katydid* steamed into St Louis. Tad never saw her, but he knew the moment she arrived. Everyone with a bet on the *Omaha* went racing off to fetch Esther and Mr Jackson.

They appeared in the middle of a crowd, being hustled along the wharf at top speed. Miss Whitwell watched in silence, standing stiff and upright beside Tad. As they came closer, scraps of talk floated up to the boiler deck.

'There weren't two boys with it. Just the one . . . '

'Little fellow. With a squeaky voice.'

Esther's feathers bobbed above the crowd, and her voice sliced through the muttering. 'I *told* you to forget about Tad! He hasn't got the sense to get here on his own.'

Tad hardly noticed. He was used to Esther. But there was a strange, suppressed snort above his head and he looked up to see Miss Whitwell staring towards the stage plank with narrowed eyes.

A moment or two later, the stage was hauled in and a cloud

of steam hissed into the air. With a roar from the wharf, and a shout of triumph from every deck, the *City of Omaha* headed out into the river.

From St Louis to Kansas City it was almost four hundred miles. Two and a half days, with the wild, brown water racing against them all the way.

Tad crouched in his corner, watching the shore for ribbons, and Miss Whitwell patrolled the boat, striding from deck to deck with her boots clacking on the wet planks and her skirts swirling. When Tad least expected it, she would appear at his elbow, bringing him something to eat, or a mug of thick Missouri water.

And she always knew exactly what was going on in the boat.

'It's safe to walk now. Jackson's up in the pilot-house, annoying the pilot. And That Woman has got herself into a card game.'

'I'm not sure I should—'

'Go *on*, boy! You've got to have exercise. I'll keep watch for you.'

Tad grinned and walked up and down the boat. But he didn't stop watching the shore.

Then it was a hundred miles from Kansas City to St Joseph. Fifteen hours more, and the *Omaha* was gaining all the way.

They always knew how they were doing. Every boat that came down the other way brought them news of the *Sarah Dewar*. It ran through the boat in minutes, and Miss Whitwell took it straight to Tad.

It never sounded good.

The *Sarah Dewar*'s lead shrank to three hours and then to two and a half. Miss Whitwell looked grimmer and grimmer, and once or twice Tad heard Esther crowing from one of the higher decks.

And still they steamed on, with Iowa on the right bank and

Kansas on the left. The *City of Omaha* devoured wood, like a giant eating celery, and Tad sat staring as the stokers laboured. Thinking of Khush, on the boiler deck of the other boat. How was he enduring the journey? Was Cissie bothering to wash him, and take care of his feet?

At midnight, they passed Rulo, and there was Nebraska at last, on the left hand shore. Tad peered out into the darkness, but it swirled impenetrably in front of his eyes. He rested his chin on his knees and thought about Ketty in the shade of a tall apple tree. About wide fields of corn, and creek water so clear that you could see the bottom of the mug.

Thought about anything he could. Except what he might be missing, in the dark, as they steamed along the Nebraska shore.

See where I am, Ketty—on dry land in Nebraska!

I intended to stay in St Louis and wait for Tad. I had resolved to spend several weeks there, if necessary.

But I did not know that I was being followed.

Mr Jackson (the man who is trying to steal Khush) was close behind me, and he had telegraphed ahead. When Khush and I reached St Louis, we were expected.

It seemed that we were to be kept there until Mr Jackson arrived, so that things could be sorted out. I know that kind of sorting out. I should have lost Khush for ever—and maybe my liberty as well. Even if Tad had come, he could have done nothing to save me.

But desperation brought inspiration.

Do you remember what Pa did, when we were in such straits in Maryland? He began an argument about how fast Khush could run, and then he took bets. *Once people start betting*, he always said, *someone has an interest in helping you.* And so they did, for we ran right away.

The same thing worked in St Louis. Someone was kind enough to say that I 'couldn't get far with that elephant'. 'Indeed I can!' says I. 'If Khush and I board the next boat for Omaha, it will be there before Mr Jackson!' (I chose my words with care, as you shall see.)

Immediately, the whole situation was transformed! The next boat due to sail for Omaha was a squat, ramshackle craft—the *Sarah Dewar*—but her captain was eager to bet on her speed.

And there were plenty of people to disagree with him. They hauled out the captain of the *City of Omaha* (the fastest boat available) and he agreed to wait for Mr Jackson.

And, more than that, *he* was happy to bet as well, even though he did not know how far behind he would start. He said the *Sarah Dewar* would never reach Omaha at all, if she set out with an elephant on board.

That meant that both captains were taking bets.

Then the pilots began. And people on the wharf, betting with each other. Even mothers, with babies in their arms, risked a few cents, one way or the other.

And Pa was right! Once the bets were placed, I was no longer short of friends. Dozens of people hustled me aboard the *Sarah Dewar*. Some of them even embarked with me. Within hours of reaching St Louis, Khush and I were off to Missouri, cheered to the echo by a wharf full of gamblers.

But—I had worded my bet very carefully. I *set out* on the *Sarah Dewar*, but it was never my intention to travel the whole way to Omaha. I meant to disembark secretly, once we reached Nebraska, leaving Mr Jackson to race on to Omaha in vain. And I had left a message to tell Tad how to find me—cunningly worded, so that only he could understand.

When I explained this to the captain, and to the passengers who had bet on me, they were *delighted*. Not only were they to lose several tons of cargo (thus gaining a great deal of speed) but they were getting rid of Khush. Who has been *impossible* to manage without Tad.

They put me ashore—loading me with provisions and instructions and good advice—and here I am, hiding beside a wooded creek that runs down through the bluffs.

And I cannot move. For if I do, I shall lose Tad for ever. I must hide here, hoping that he has received my message and that he has followed me.

I have hung my secret signal from the tallest tree and prayed (Out loud, Ketty! With poor Khush staring in bewilderment!) that everyone but Tad will mistake it for the laundry of some careful Nebraskan housewife.

And now I can do nothing but wait.

Chapter 25

After Tad had watched and worried for four days, aboard the *City of Omaha*, things suddenly began to happen very fast. They pulled round the Glenwood towhead, a few miles below Plattsmouth, and swept in close to the Nebraska shore. And somewhere way ahead of them they saw black smoke, heading up the river.

Immediately, the whole ship was buzzing. Even Tad, in his corner, heard the arguments . . . *surely can't be the Sarah Dewar . . . Pacific Bend . . . St Mary's Bend . . . less than two hours away . . . can't have gained so much . . .*

Frantic shouts of 'Trim the boat, there!' came from the pilot-house as passengers crowded forward to stare. Tad wriggled out of his corner to follow them, but before he could move Miss Whitwell was at his shoulder.

'Don't waste your time on the smoke!' She grabbed his arm and turned him sideways, towards the Nebraska shore. 'Have *those* got anything to do with ribbons?'

Tad looked across at the bluffs. Just opposite the boat was a wooded creek, cutting its way down to the river. Half-way down the creek, flying from the top of a tree, was an unmistakable forked flutter. A pair of fancy cotton drawers.

He was too far away to see the scarlet ribbons, but he knew they were there. No one but Cissie would fly a signal like that.

Miss Whitwell put her mouth close to his ear. 'Can you swim?' He nodded, and she beamed at him. 'There's your chance, then. You can go over the side while they're all gawping at that smoke.'

Tad glanced backwards, at the stokers, and she grinned.

'I can take care of *them*. I'll go over to the other side of the boat—and faint.'

She said it gleefully, shaking her silly ringlets at him. And

Tad knew she would do it. She wouldn't think anything of making a fool of herself, if it helped him to get away.

'You're too good, ma'am. I don't know how—'

Miss Whitwell flushed, ducking her head to avoid his thanks. 'Stuff! I'd have gone mad on this trip, without you. I would have sat in a corner, all by myself, worrying about whether William Ellicott would take to me.'

'If he doesn't take to you, he's an idiot!' Tad said fiercely. 'And if *you* don't take to *him*, you turn straight round and leave him standing. You deserve the best!'

He bobbed forward and kissed her hard on her thin, dry cheek. She spluttered, putting a hand to her face, and for a moment he was afraid he had offended her.

And then she smiled. Not her schoolboy grin, but a straightforward, happy smile. With one finger, she brushed Tad's chin and tapped him on the end of the nose. Then she stumped off across the deck, to the further rail.

Quietly, Tad slipped off his boots and tied the laces together. Then he watched. Miss Whitwell waited until there was another puff of smoke and the noise from the front of the boat grew louder. Then, with a little shriek, she crumpled and fell awkwardly to the deck, hitting the boards with an inelegant thump. All the stokers turned towards her, one or two of them running to help, and the rest sniggering openly.

Tad slung his boots round his neck, slipped quietly over the side and began to swim towards the Nebraska bluffs.

He was still several yards from the shore when he heard a shrill squeal. Familiar and unmistakable. Khush came charging out of the trees and plunged straight into the river.

Tad looked round anxiously, but the *Omaha* was almost round the bend, and every soul on board was staring straight ahead, towards the smoke of the *Sarah Dewar*. There was no one to see, as Tad and Khush met each other, in deep water, face to face.

Tad flung his arms round the huge head and felt Khush's trunk go tight round his waist. They'd done it. They were together again. Leaning his face against the top of the trunk, Tad knew that he'd never expected it to happen. He'd never expected to feel that rough patch of skin, ever again.

Khush carried him in, towards the river bank, and lifted him out of the water. Tad lay on the shore, without moving, watching Khush scramble up after him. Watching the way his body moved, the lovely, familiar, wrinkled patterns of his skin.

'Hallo?' said an uncertain voice, from under the trees.

Turning, Tad peered into the shadows. He couldn't see her, but he could smell the woodsmoke from her fire. 'Cissie?'

And then she was there. She threw herself down the slope and flung her arms round him.

'Oh, you're here, you're *here*! I can't believe it! I never really thought you would—I'm sorry I didn't do what you said! I'm sorry I didn't wait for you—'

'I—' Tad was overwhelmed. He looked down at the cropped head pressed against his chest. 'You'll get wet.'

'Who cares about a bit of water?' She hugged him again, hard, and then began to drag him up the slope, towards her fire.

Close to the creek, the trees thinned. Cissie had built a small fire on some stones and it was glowing red, almost burnt out.

'They gave me some cornmeal when they put me off the *Sarah Dewar*. And a lump of bacon. I've been making ash cakes.'

She began to rake the fire apart. Underneath the embers were four flat cakes, wrapped in scorched leaves. She lifted them out with two sticks and laid them on a stone in front of Tad.

'There you are. I saved some for you. I *knew* you'd come.'

That wasn't what she had said a moment before, but the message was the same. She was overjoyed to see him. Tad squatted down beside her and started to pull the leaves away, licking his fingers to stop them being burnt. Inside were four little cornmeal cakes. He broke a piece off one, blew on it and put it in his mouth.

'That's good.'

'Not the sort of food polite folks care for,' Cissie said.

Tad chewed the cake carefully. It wasn't a match for Miss Whitwell's pecan pie, but it was warm and wholesome. 'Where did you learn to make ash cakes?'

'When I was five, we travelled with a circus. Pa and Ketty and me and Olivia. That was where Pa bought Khush. There was a half-breed in the circus. Used to dress up like a Cherokee and do an arrow turn.'

She glanced up and grinned at Tad as he put another piece in his mouth. Then she went on.

'Johnny knew a thing or two his mother had taught him, before his pa carried him off east, to be a white man. He had a neat hand with the ash cakes, but there was no one who cared to eat them. Only me—and Olivia.'

She stared into the embers and, for a moment, Tad caught the picture of her strange, wandering life. He could almost see the two little girls, sitting round that other fire, with a circus Indian.

No place had ever been home for Cissie. Only people. And now Olivia was dead. And Michael Keenan was dead. And Cissie was sitting by another fire, in Nebraska, with no one to call family but a Swedish farmer's wife.

And an orphan boy from Markle, who always did things wrong.

Tad swallowed. 'Cissie—'

He didn't know what he was going to say. What he might not have said. But Cissie wasn't looking at him. She was still staring into the fire.

'We could do with Johnny now. To help us get to Ketty's. I'm not sure we can manage on our own.'

Tad blinked. 'I thought we were almost there.'

'So did I. I counted on making it before Mr Jackson caught the *Sarah Dewar*. But I met a man on the boat. Used to have a quarter section in Nebraska, until his wife died.'

'And?'

Cissie scooped a handful of water from the creek and threw it on to the fire, so that the embers hissed and spat.

158

'There's another two hundred miles to go. And no way to travel but walking.'

She looked up suddenly and Tad realized how thin her face had grown. Not a child's face at all. Esther's words came slicing back into his brain. *You'll never manage, west of the Mississippi . . . that elephant will die . . . Cissie's too old to be travelling round with a boy like you . . .*

The familiar feeling of hopeless, clumsy stupidity welled up, pushing him towards despair. *Remember how young you are . . . how prone to disasters . . .*

But Cissie was staring at him, waiting for what he would say. This time, there was no room for despair. If he gave up hope, she would give up, too.

'Don't worry,' he said, firmly. 'We're going to make it. And if that means walking, we'll walk.'

She grabbed his hands and held them hard. 'You're sure?'

'I'm sure. You're going to get to Ketty's.' Tad loosened her grip and put her hands gently back in her lap. Then he said it again, making a promise. 'You're going to get safe to Ketty's.'

159

CHAPTER 26

THEY BEGAN to walk as soon as the night was dark enough
to hide them, stumbling and slithering on the rough trail,
with only a lantern to light the ground. In an hour, they were
looking down on Plattsmouth.

Tad stopped, studying the neat grid of streets and the
buildings scattered further up the valley. The streets were
dark, but there were dozens of bright windows, especially
down by the river.

'Let's see the map.'

The man on the *Sarah Dewar* had sketched the route for
Cissie, on the back of a crumpled piece of paper. Tad
smoothed it out and huddled close to the lantern, trying to
make out the scrawled lines.

'We have to get past Plattsmouth, so that we can cross the
Platte river. We must do that before it's light.'

Cissie put her head close to his, peering at the map. 'The
man said we should follow the railroad tracks along the river.
They'll bring us to the bridge.'

'If we go that way now, we'll be seen.' Tad frowned down at
the lights in Plattsmouth. 'Maybe we ought to go round the
back of the town.'

'I *can't*.' Cissie snatched the map back and began to fold it
up. In the shadows of the lantern light, her wrists were thin
and frail, with the bones sticking out in great knobs.

Tad looked at her. Then he looked at Khush. At his
drooping, baggy skin, and the way he avoided putting his
weight on one back foot.

'All right,' he said. 'We'll go the quickest way we can. But
we'll have to wait until the lights go out.'

They settled themselves, staring down at Plattsmouth.
Cissie curled up on the ground, with her arms round her legs
and her head on her knees. Tad sat beside her, very still. And

Khush blundered badtemperedly round them, nudging Tad with his trunk and snatching mouthfuls of grass. Below them, very, very slowly, the lights began to flicker out.

It must have been two or three in the morning when the last one disappeared. Cissie had dropped into a doze and Khush was asleep, lying flat out on the ground. Tad knelt to mutter in his ear.

'Get up, Khush.'

The great, slack body stirred. One eye opened and looked up shrewdly.

'Time to go,' Tad said.

With a heave, Khush was on his feet, flapping his ears and gazing round warily. Tad tapped Cissie on the shoulder.

'Time to go.'

'What? I—' She blinked, stretched and stood up. 'Is it safe now?'

'We'll have to be very quiet. There's sure to be some kind of watchman down by the railroad depot.'

Cissie nodded and slapped Khush on the side. 'Come on. Off we go.'

The railroad ran below the bluffs, very close to the river and right along the front of the town. As they drew near to the dark buildings, Cissie leaned closer to Khush and whispered, 'Creep, Khush. Creep.'

Khush began to lift his heavy feet and place them down completely silently, without knocking a stone or breaking a stick. It was ridiculous to watch—a circus turn without an audience—but it carried him soundlessly along the railroad.

He slid past Plattsmouth like a giant shadow, with two smaller shadows trailing him. The wind was coming from the west, off the high ground, and it carried his scent away from the town and over the river. No dogs stirred. No windows lit up. There would not be a soul to tell Mr Jackson that an elephant had gone by.

It was an hour before they were properly past the town, and another two hours before they reached the railroad bridge. By the time they got there, the sky was beginning to lighten, very faintly.

They stood and gazed across the grey expanse of the Platte, watching the mist move on its surface. The bridge looked very long and very exposed.

'We have to do it now?' Cissie said.

'Now,' Tad said firmly. It didn't occur to him that he was giving orders. He just knew that they had to get across and out of sight.

Khush sidled away from them, down towards the water.

'No!' Cissie said. But she sounded weary.

'Let him go,' said Tad. 'He'll come, when he sees us on the other side.'

Cissie looked at the bridge again. 'It's a long way.'

'But when we're across, we're well on the way to Ketty's. Come on.'

Tad pulled her after him, on to the bridge. Their feet slipped on the damp sleepers and once or twice Cissie caught her toe in the ballast and pitched forward on to her knees. But she scrambled up again and kept walking, mechanically, looking back at Khush every now and again.

He came after them when they were half-way over, just as Tad had known he would. They heard the thump of his heavy feet on the timbers and by the time they reached the opposite bank he was right behind them. Walking close to Tad, as if he were afraid of losing him again.

'Only a few miles more tonight,' Tad said cheerfully. 'If we go up the Platte, we're sure to find a creek where we can shelter. And sleep.'

'Fine.'

Cissie turned left and began to stump along the river bank, stumbling and staggering. Tad followed. There was no need to give any order to Khush. He stayed close behind, reaching out, every now and again, to touch Tad with the tip of his trunk.

As the sun rose, they reached a little wooded valley where a creek came down to the river. There was a house a mile or so up the creek, where the ground rose towards the open prairie, but there were plenty of trees to hide them while they slept for a few hours.

'Here,' said Cissie. She slipped the bundle off her back, rolled herself in one of the blankets and was instantly asleep, tucked in between two bushes.

Tad stood for a moment, gazing down at her. Curled into her blanket, with the ragged hair tumbled round her face, she looked like a small, grubby boy, frowning in his sleep.

He glanced at Khush. 'Stay here. Look after Cissie.'

Khush rumbled in his stomach.

'It's all right,' Tad said gently. 'I'm coming back.'

There was another rumble. But then Khush turned away and pulled a trunkful of grass. Tad grinned and started to climb up, out of the creek bottom.

He skirted the farmhouse, without being seen, and climbed until he was beyond the trees. Then he stood still, looking out across the beginning of the prairie.

Afterwards, he never knew what it was that he had expected. A mish-mash of things he had heard was churning in his head. *The prairies are like the sea . . . herds of buffalo . . . farmland for everyone . . . the Great American Desert . . .* He had imagined the river flats at Markle, blown up to a grand scale. A neat pattern of fields, with houses scattered along the back roads. Buffalo grazing like cows in lush, green meadows.

He hadn't understood at all.

Ahead of him, as far as he could see, was a great expanse of flat land, completely unmarked by anything that people could do to it. Houses, cattle, fields—they were all insignificant on the surface of that huge emptiness. It was bigger than anything he could possibly have imagined, stretching away to the west in a vast, unbroken sweep. No trees. No shelter. No corners to hide in.

Tad stood on the edge of it and stared, with his heart thumping, not knowing whether he was excited or afraid. That was where they were heading. And somewhere, out in the middle of that empty plain, was Ketty's house.

He put his hand into his pocket and felt the smooth shape of the little glass bottle that he had carried such a long way.

Maple Creek
13th May

We are almost with you!

But you must not think it has been easy. We have crossed the Platte and struggled north and west, up the Elkhorn Valley and along Maple Creek—on our *own feet*, because Tad is too careful of Khush's sore heels to let us ride. Tad estimates (having talked *at length* with every farmer we have encountered) that we have walked over a hundred miles already.

He is the one who has brought us through. When I want to give up too soon, he persuades me to walk further, and when I persevere foolishly, he makes me rest. And he will not say anything to dampen my spirits.

I know he worries about being followed, for he glances over his shoulder constantly. But he will not share his anxiety with me. Sometimes I wish he would, for that keeps a kind of distance between us, but it is no use to ask. He never speaks of his own feelings.

In any case, I cannot believe that Mr Jackson will find us now. We have avoided the obvious route, along the Platte valley, and have gone north up its tributaries, into wilder and less settled country. Surely news cannot travel over spaces like this? It seems impossible that the inhabitants should know even who is President.

As we pass, they tumble from their houses and stare at Khush with wide, incredulous eyes. The children are barefoot. The women are lined and brown-skinned. The men are silent creatures of every tongue—German and Dutch and Swedish being the most common—who come from their fields covered in mud, to grunt a few words at Tad.

They are fascinated by Khush, but mainly because they consider him as an animal who might, perhaps, be of use to farming on the prairies. Me, for the most part, they ignore entirely, as being a younger brother, of no account. One or two of the women, maybe, have noticed that I am not what I seem, but their natural hospitality (and preoccupation with their own affairs) prevents them from meddling.

And what hospitality it is! We have but to appear with Khush, and the best that they can offer is laid before us. Corn chowder and bean stew. Spoon bread and vinegar pie. All that is ever asked in return is an elephant ride for the children, or Khush's help with hauling logs. (And Khush does whatever Tad asks of him.) This place makes Baltimore seem an impossibly foreign land, but I am beginning to think kindly of it, all the same.

I could live here and be happy, Ketty. If only you will keep me. Once Khush is sold, I shall be able to pay my way. And perhaps pay for Tad too.

Oh, say you will let me stay, dear Ketty! Let me live with you, and make a fresh start!

Then I shall be able to forget everything that happened on that terrible train.

CHAPTER 27

ON THE seventh day, the thing that Tad had been afraid of happened for the first time.

They were heading due west, across the prairies north of Maple Creek, hoping to hit a farm round about sunset. They trudged steadily for the first half of the day, and coaxed Khush through the second half, when he was hungry and beginning to limp more.

Tad saw the farmhouse when they were still a couple of miles away. It stood on a slight rise, a fine, big house made of dirt bricks cut from the ground around it. As they walked towards it, he was preparing the words he would say when they arrived. *Good evening. We're walking west with our elephant . . .*

But he didn't need them. When they were still half a mile away, they saw a small, bonneted figure walk out of the house and look towards them, with her hands on her hips. The next moment, she was shrieking so loudly that they could hear her clear across the distance in between.

'E-li-jah! They're here!'

Then she picked up her skirts and came scurrying towards them, setting up a dust all around her. In front raced a little black dog, who reached them first. He danced round Khush, barking hysterically.

'Stop that, Puck!' the girl snapped, as she caught up with him. She grabbed the dog by the scruff of its neck and pulled it away. 'Stupid animal! You'll burst a blood vessel, carrying on like that!'

She was hardly older than Tad. Sixteen, at the most, with her hair wrenched back into a braided bun, to make her look grown up. Her face was pink with excitement as she stood there, holding the dog.

'My husband was right. Said you'd be here before the day

was out. Well, you're very welcome. All three of you.'

Tad tried to smile politely. 'Your—your husband knew we were coming?'

The girl let go of the dog and dusted off her hands. 'Certainly did. Drove back from Columbus yesterday, with the stores, and couldn't talk about anything else. How there was an elephant on the prairie and folks reckoned it was coming up Maple Creek.' She turned round and yelled again. 'E-LI-JAH!'

A tall man came round from behind the farmhouse and looked across at them. The girl beckoned impatiently.

'Dang the man! He just has to take his time about everything he does. Even when it's a sight like this.' She stared up, admiringly, at Khush, who was busy pulling grass and stuffing it into his mouth. 'Let's go and meet him.'

She slapped the dog on its rump and it raced back towards the farmer, jumping round his legs when it reached him. The girl shook her head.

'Worst behaved dog I ever saw. Elijah hasn't got a notion how to train 'em.'

She started back briskly and, behind her back, Tad pulled a face at Cissie.

'They knew about us,' he hissed. 'It must be all up and down the Platte Valley by now. Mr Jackson's sure to hear.'

Cissie shrugged. 'What can we do? We have to keep going, and hope we reach Ketty's before they catch us.'

'But—'

But what difference will that make? Tad thought the words, but he didn't say them. He let Cissie wander on, towards the farmhouse, and he followed with Khush.

The girl who had greeted them was back with her husband now, hanging on his arm and chattering as she pointed towards Khush. She was excited and the dog was excited. Even the chickens clucking round their feet were excited. But the man was calm. He was much older than she was—maybe twenty years older—and he looked amused.

As Tad reached them, the girl stepped back and shook her head, grinning with exasperation.

167

'Aren't you even going to take a *look*? Elijah Davenport, you are the most provoking man I have ever met!'

Elijah laughed then, and turned to Tad. 'You're very welcome. Both of you, and your elephant. I guess I have to meet the creature *this very minute*, or Amy will bite off my nose.'

He looked past Tad at Khush, who was lumbering the last few yards towards them, with his eyes fixed on Tad. The little dog began to yap again, but Elijah glared and he fell silent, cowering back on his haunches and whimpering slightly.

'He's a good dog,' Elijah said absently, 'but he's never seen an elephant before. I've never seen one as big as yours myself. But I expected it, from what they said in Columbus. A big Indian elephant. Travelling west with—a couple of boys.'

He glanced briefly at Cissie, and Tad knew that he had heard about her, too. But he obviously hadn't told Amy. She looked all three of them over in the same cheerfully scornful way and pointed at the house.

'A couple of *starving* boys, I reckon. Why don't you stop jawing and get that animal tethered. Then you can come inside and eat.'

Elijah looked at Khush. 'Reckon he'll be all right out here?'

'What are you frightened of? Wolves? Eagles?' Amy snorted. 'There's not one of them would dare to touch *him*. You get him fixed up over there and I'll take Puck inside and fix the supper.'

Elijah hesitated. 'I was thinking of the cold—'

Amy tilted her head and spread out her hand, feeling the air. Then she shook her head firmly. 'No frost tonight. Put him close to the house, round on the far side, and he'll be fine.'

She grabbed the dog again and hauled him inside, leaving Elijah to deal with Khush. He stood and watched as Tad and Cissie tethered him and he showed them where to find water.

'Drinks a fair bit, doesn't he?' he commented, after the sixth bucketful. 'He could be in for a hard time out here. Not all the creeks last right round the year, like this one.'

Tad felt a shiver at the back of his neck, but all he said was,

'We're not going much further. We hoped you could show us a trail going west. Towards Looking Glass Creek.'

'No use asking me.' Elijah chuckled. 'I've only been here a few years. It's Amy you want.'

Cissie blinked. 'We do?'

Elijah nodded. 'She was born out here. Lived through the grasshopper summer of '74. Sucked in prairie farming with her mother's milk. Marrying her was the best day's work I ever did.' He smiled his slow smile, and looked at Khush. 'Is he settled now?'

'When I tell him where we're going.' Tad put a hand on Khush's side, to catch his attention, and then he pointed at the farmhouse. 'We're going there. You're staying here, until we come to fetch you.'

'You think that means anything? To a dumb animal?' Cissie shook her head at him.

But it seemed to. Khush flapped his ears and took a long look at the farmhouse. Then he bent his head to the grass they had cut for him, and when they walked off he didn't take any notice. Tad saw Elijah grin quietly to himself.

By the time they reached the farmhouse, Amy had a fine supper laid out on the table. A great pot of beans and sowbelly and a dish of dandelion greens, wilted in bacon dripping.

'You can wash over there,' she said briskly. 'Hurry up now. and sit yourselves down. No point in letting good food go cold.'

She waited until they were all round the table, and then looked expectantly at Elijah.

'O Lord,' Elijah said comfortably, 'look kindly on this meal of ours. You know how hard we worked to get the makings of it. We're grateful that our work bore fruit, and that we have food to set in front of these visitors. Please bless it, and all of us who eat it. Amen.'

'Amen,' Amy said, beginning to serve out the beans before the word was out of her mouth.

Elijah settled himself on his chair. 'These boys here reckon they want to strike west. To Looking Glass Creek. I told them they ought to talk to you about the trail.'

169

Amy grinned and shook her head at him. 'If they've been listening to you, they'll expect me to know every place in Nebraska. I've never been as far west as Looking Glass Creek.'

'But you know the trail.' Elijah picked a piece of meat off his plate and fed it to Puck, ignoring Amy's frown. 'You could put them on their way.'

'Oh, I know the *trail*, right enough. Pa used to go hunting out that way. He always said it was easy to follow. It'll take them clear through to Beaver Creek, if they need to go that far. But they'll need to carry water with them.'

'What about the creeks?' Tad said quickly.

'You can't count on the little ones.'

'But Khush—' Tad thought of all the buckets of water he had just carried up for him.

'It won't hurt Khush to go thirsty for an hour or two,' Cissie said, interrupting. She pulled the crumpled map out of her pocket and spread it on the table. 'Would you mark the trail on here for us?'

She and Amy bent over the paper, their heads close together. Tad saw Amy frown, muttering as she marked the map. It wasn't going to be an easy journey, even without the threat of Mr Jackson behind them.

Cissie's face was stubborn. She jabbed at the map with her finger, insisting on something. Determined to have her own way, even after all she had been through. Tad grinned.

Then he looked up and found Elijah watching him. Watching him watching Cissie.

Scooping the last piece of meat from his plate, Tad forked it into his mouth. *Ketty*, he thought, childishly. *Things will be simple when we get to Ketty's*. And the cool, green shadows danced in his brain, like impossible desires.

CHAPTER 28

THEY LEFT late the next morning. In return for their food, and the night's shelter, Tad took Khush along the creek to haul timber for Elijah, while Cissie stayed at the farmhouse, splitting wood.

'Amy hoped you would help me out,' Elijah said, in his slow, amused voice, as he and Tad walked along behind Khush. 'The moment she heard you were on your way, she had a thousand jobs to suggest, if you offered.'

Tad grinned, and put a hand on the ropes round Khush's shoulders. 'Seems like you all need elephants out here.'

'We need a special kind.' Elijah grinned wryly. 'One that can stand cold in the winter. And drought and blazing sun in the summer. You reckon yours could cope with that?'

Tad grinned and shrugged, but the question wouldn't go away. It bothered him all the time he and Khush were hauling wood, and it was still niggling away at the back of his mind when the time came to leave.

It was after midday when Amy put them on the trail. She cooked up a skillet full of hootsla for lunch, beating up a dozen eggs to go with the fried bread cubes, and when it was all eaten she took off her apron and hung it up on the back of the door.

Then she fetched two battered kerosene cans from the barn.

'You'd best take these with you. You can fill them again, whenever you get the chance. There's fifty miles to travel, and it's going to be warm.'

Cissie filled the cans and slung them over Khush's neck, behind what remained of their bundle of food. Amy nodded approvingly.

'Let's get going. I'll take you as far as the start of the trail.'

Elijah shook their hands and wished them good luck, and they set off, going north-west until they crossed the trail. They would never have found it without Amy. She stopped suddenly, in the middle of the open prairie, and pointed due west.

'See it? It's clear all the way like that, Pa said. You shouldn't have any trouble. Just make sure you stop for the night while you can still see the trail.'

There was nothing but a line of dark grass, worn shorter than all the rest and stretching away towards the horizon. Cissie looked at Tad, and raised her eyebrows.

Amy caught the look. 'You'll be fine. Gather up cow chips as you go, and you'll have something to light a fire with when it's dark. That should keep off any wolves.'

Cissie pulled a face, but Tad nudged her into silence. He held out a hand. 'We're obliged to you for your hospitality. There's just one more favour we'd like to ask—'

'Ask what you like,' Amy said. 'But there's not much we can do for anyone.'

'We don't need much. Only—' Tad hesitated. 'Please don't tell anyone which way we've gone.'

Amy looked at him, considering. But she didn't ask any questions. Just nodded at Khush.

'He's done more work than the horse could do in three days. I reckon we owe you something.'

'Thank you, ma'am.'

'You're welcome. Goodbye.'

She stared up at Khush once more, as if she were fixing him in her memory. Then she nodded at Tad and Cissie and turned back the way she had come. They stood and watched her as she headed off towards the farm. A small, tough figure, striding through the prairie grass.

'I like her,' Cissie said, abruptly. 'And she's not too far away from Ketty's.'

The future opened up, suddenly, in Tad's head, like a great, black gulf. Until then, the journey had stretched on and on in his mind, as though there would never be anything but travelling. As though he and Cissie and Khush could spend the rest of their lives walking west. But it was almost over. In two or three days, they would be at Ketty's.

And then what?

Emptiness gaped in his brain.

'Let's get going,' he said roughly. 'We ought to make ten or twelve miles before dark. Move up, Khush.'

All that day, and all the next day, they walked until they were exhausted. Then they stopped on the open prairie, making a small, smouldering fire of dried animal droppings.

But Tad didn't sleep.

Each evening he cooked a few ash cakes and bullied Cissie into eating some of them. Then he watched as she rolled herself up in her blanket by the fire.

She slept instantly, with her arm curled under her head and the blanket pulled over her shoulders, but she didn't look peaceful. In the firelight, Tad saw her frowning and fretting in her sleep, as though her dreams disturbed her. Her thin, tired face twisted unhappily, with the eyes tightly shut.

Everything will come right when we get to Ketty's.

Tad tried hard to go on believing that. But, even now, he wasn't sure they would make it.

They were travelling through empty land, where lots of the farms were abandoned, but there were still too many people around, taking notice of them.

On the first day, there was a man, way off on the horizon, driving a buggy. Then, when they crossed Shell Creek, they spoke to two women down by the water. And, late on in the second day, they met a whole group of farmers, working on a new barn.

Every one of those people had seen Khush, and a story like that was too good to waste. All over Nebraska, people must be talking about the elephant on the prairie.

The word was bound to reach Mr Jackson, before long.

Tad lay gazing up at the great, open dome of the sky, trying to see into the future. Behind him, Khush rambled about, sometimes eating, and sometimes lying down to sleep. When he came close, his body was like a wall, shutting out the stars. But when he moved, there was no shelter. Nothing to shield Tad from the black, empty spaces of the universe.

By the end of the second night, Tad was light-headed with fatigue. Cissie had to pull him on to his feet to get him going.

'Come on! If we get across Looking Glass Creek by midday, we should be there before dark. Eat this, and we can go.'

This was a cold, scorched ashcake, left over from the night before. Tad choked it down, and reached for one of the kerosene-smelling cans that they had filled at the last creek.

But Khush was before him. He came sidling up, tweaked the can away and lifted it high into the air.

'No!' Tad shouted.

But Khush was very thirsty. He hadn't drunk his fill since they left Maple Creek. Raising the can high in the air, he smashed it down hard on to the ground and squashed it flat with one foot. Then, before the pool of water could run into the dry ground, he had sucked it up and squirted it into his mouth.

'Khush!' Cissie said fiercely.

But he hadn't finished. Pushing Cissie out of the way, he snatched up the other can.

There was no way of stopping him. It would have been foolish to try. He towered high above them both, whirling the can over their heads. Then he smashed it down, right at Tad's feet, and sucked up the water.

Tad looked down at the damp patch on the grass and into his mind, irresistibly, came the thought of Ketty, sitting on the porch of the white frame house.

The flowers in the garden fluttered beneath the great, green leaves of the trees, and the breeze blew fresh and gentle. As fresh as the noise of water running over stones in the Tamaquon valley.

'Come on,' he muttered, feeling the dryness in his throat. 'We'll just have to go as fast as we can. Move up, Khush.'

Slowly, the three of them began. They were all limping slightly now, and Khush dragged his feet, looking guiltily at Tad as he walked. But Tad hadn't got the energy to be angry.

174

He just concentrated on putting his feet one in front of the other.

There had been a slight frost in the night, and every blade of grass was edged with white. They trailed across it, leaving a wide, damp track behind them. Now that Tad was accustomed to the featureless, rolling spread of the prairie, the track stood out like an arrow, pointing the way they had gone.

Until midday, they walked more or less steadily, crawling across the land with nothing but the dark green trail to guide them. Khush fell further and further behind, dragging and dawdling as his feet began to hurt more. By the time they reached the creek, Tad and Cissie were almost half a mile ahead.

And when Khush reached the creek, he wouldn't leave it. It was very low, but he stood stubbornly in the middle of the creek bottom, with his feet in the water, drinking and drinking.

Cissie stamped her foot. 'Idiot! Stupid elephant! Don't you know we're nearly there? Another couple of hours at the most. And then we'll be with Ketty!'

Khush didn't even raise his head.

Cissie looked up at the bundles. 'There's only one thing for it. Where did we put the bullhook?'

Tad remembered Khush's rage that morning. He was as tired and irritable as they were. Ready to explode at any moment. Grabbing Cissie's shoulder, Tad pulled her back.

'Not the bullhook. It's not safe. He'll follow us if we go on.'

'But we can't just leave him—'

'Come on.' Tad pulled her up the bank, until they were standing on the prairie, looking down into the creek bottom. Then he called, sharply. 'We're going, Khush. Come here!'

Khush lifted his head and stood staring at them.

'Come *on!*' Tad said.

Still holding Cissie's hand, he began to drag her across the prairie, pulling her into a run.

'But suppose he doesn't—' she panted. 'I can't—'

Tad looked back over his shoulder. They hadn't come far, but Khush was completely invisible now, hidden down by the creek. And the gap was widening all the time.

'Keep running!' he said urgently.

'But—I've got to have Khush—you don't understand—I need—'

'Cissie, you have to come with me!'

He tugged her again, and then they were running hand in hand, keeping pace with each other. The gap widened to a hundred yards, and then to a quarter of a mile.

When they were half a mile away from the creek, Tad glanced back again, and saw Khush's head. He had climbed just far enough up the bank to see where they were.

'Come on!' he panted. 'It's working!'

Somewhere, further away, towards the horizon, beyond Khush, his eye caught a movement. An irregularity in the great, flat sweep of the plain. But he was too busy to work out what it was. They had to keep running.

The next time he looked back, Khush had climbed right out on to the prairie. He stood very still, dwarfed by the enormous empty space around him. And beyond him, the moving figures that Tad had almost noticed before began to move faster.

Two horses, that had been walking, began to gallop.

'Tad!' shrieked Cissie. 'Look! We've got to—'

She pulled at his hand, trying to go back, but at that moment Khush began to move. He seemed to make up his mind all at once, and he started charging towards them, at full speed.

For one, agonizing second, Tad thought of the weight thudding down on to that poor, split heel. Then he ran on, dragging Cissie after him. 'Keep moving!'

'But the horses—'

'If we stop, Khush will stop, too. If he keeps running, we might—'

They were so *close* to Ketty's. For two thousand miles they had dodged and hidden and escaped, and they'd almost made it. But he knew what the horses meant. They were still tiny

176

and indistinct, but Tad could almost see Esther's purple feathers, and Mr Jackson's square body sitting heavily in the saddle. They must be the riders. The horses had begun to gallop instantly when Khush appeared out of the creek.

Was it all going to be for nothing?

Tad and Cissie kept racing on across the plain, as Khush gained on them, and the dots behind grew closer and closer. Cissie was panting desperately, and Tad's lungs felt ready to burst, but they kept up their pace, trying to stay free for as long as they could.

It took Tad some time to notice what was in front of them. Nearer than the horizon. A long, black stovepipe was sticking up through the ground, with a wisp of smoke curling idly from the top.

A chimney?

Cissie saw the pipe too, and before Tad could make any sense of it, she was yelling, gasping for breath as she ran.

'Help! Is there anyone there?'

Something stirred, and she yelled again.

'Help!'

From behind the chimney, apparently out of the ground, came a tall woman in a faded dress. She stared towards them for a second and then began to run.

The whole prairie whirled round Tad. He was running. Cissie was running at his side. Khush was lumbering after them, so close now that they could hear his feet thudding on the hard ground. And the woman was running in front, and the two horses were galloping behind.

For a second, light-headed with thirst and hunger and exhaustion, Tad felt as though they would all meet in one great collision. Smash into each other and explode into dust, blowing away across the prairie.

Then, from beside him, Cissie gave a huge shriek.

'KETTY!'

She wrenched her hand away from Tad and raced ahead, flinging herself into the arms of the lined, brown, woman.

Ketty?

Tad's head spun. He had come two thousand miles. Down

the Ohio, up the Mississippi, along the Missouri and over the Platte. To look for a beautiful woman in a green garden.

And there was nothing. Just another plain, brown, woman in faded calico, like any other farmer's wife. No golden hair. No white frame house. And no cool, green garden. As far as he could see, Ketty had crawled out of a hole in the ground.

They were in the middle of nowhere, with their enemies close behind—and there was no one to save them. Tad hadn't realized what childish, magical hope he had been cherishing. Until that moment, when he staggered to a stop in the prairie dust and waited for Mr Jackson and Esther to catch them.

But Cissie was clinging to Ketty as if she were a fairy godmother. Hugging her, and gasping, and babbling nonsense.

'Here, Ketty—you've got to—oh, it's hard to explain—' She looked over her shoulder and caught her breath when she saw the galloping horses, only a few hundred yards away. 'It's too much—I can't—'

Pushing her hand into the pocket of her trousers, she pulled out a battered bundle. Tad recognized the papers she had scribbled at all through their journey. Fiercely, Cissie pushed the bundle into Ketty's hand. Then, for the first time since Tad had known her, she burst into tears.

Ketty held the papers firmly in one hand and put the other arm round Cissie's shoulders. Her weatherbeaten face, gazing down at Cissie, lit up, suddenly, with a mixture of such amazement and tenderness that Tad couldn't bear it. He looked away, towards the two galloping riders, who were just reining in their horses.

And Khush sidled up and slipped his trunk over Tad's shoulder, tweaking his earlobe.

CHAPTER 29

KETTY WOULDN'T let any of them speak until she had read Cissie's letter. Tad couldn't see how she did it, for she said nothing at all. She simply walked up and down with her head bent, holding the paper in both hands. But Esther and Mr Jackson slid down from their horses, looked at each other, and waited in silence until she had finished.

Once, she stopped and stood very still for a moment, with her eyes closed. Then she glanced round at Cissie. But Cissie shook her head almost angrily.

'Not *now!*'

With a nod, Ketty went on reading.

Twice, Mr Jackson opened his mouth to interrupt, but she stopped him with a look and a movement of her hand. It was only a tiny movement, but it kept him waiting. They all stood motionless, in the middle of the prairie, watching a thin, shabby woman reading some crumpled sheets of paper.

At last, she folded the bundle of papers together and called over her shoulder, towards the stovepipe.

'Hjalmar!'

A blond head appeared beside the pipe and gradually, a tall man rose up out of the ground. Ketty smiled at him.

'*Här är Cissie och Khush,*' she said. And then, to everyone else, 'Shall we go into the house?'

Mr Jackson frowned. 'I don't know who you are, ma'am, but it's of no concern to me. All I want is my elephant. He belongs to me, and I've got the papers to prove it.'

'It's not true!' Cissie shouted. 'Pa would never have sold Khush! He's mine!'

Ketty put an arm round her shoulders. 'What you feel, Cissie, is not always what is so. It is time that we talk.'

'But—'

179

'You will please come inside. And your friend Tad, too. And this lady and gentleman.'

She waved them towards the chimney pipe. It was a hospitable gesture, but one that expected to be obeyed . . .

'Do you mean us to go *underground*?' Esther gave an elaborate shiver.

Mr Jackson shook his head. 'I wasn't born yesterday. I'm not taking my eyes off that elephant, ma'am. Not now that I've found him.'

'Khush can be tethered,' Ketty said calmly. 'He will be happy to rest, after running so far. And all of us will go inside.' She looked across at her husband. '*Låt oss gå in.*'

He nodded, and ducked down into the ground. Mr Jackson smiled sourly.

'Is there some reason for us to trust you?'

Ketty looked at him. That was all, but Tad saw his eyes flicker away sideways, backing down.

'I didn't mean to offend you, Mrs—'

'Svensson,' Ketty said, icily.

'Mrs Svensson. Of course, we'll be happy to accept your hospitality. Once the elephant's tethered.'

Ketty nodded coldly at him. Then she turned to Tad and smiled. 'You can take Khush down there, past the house. There is a little creek.'

Mr Jackson and Esther both followed, closely and suspiciously, as Tad took Khush past the stovepipe chimney and down a slope to the creek. They watched while he drove two stakes into the ground and tethered Khush, leaving him a little slack rope so that he could wade out into the water.

When that was done, Tad looked up and muttered, 'I'm going with Ketty. Stay here, Khush.'

He turned towards the dugout.

From the creek, it seemed more like a house, with a front wall made of dirt bricks and a single small window, with four panes of glass in it. But it ran back into the slope, and the roof was level with the higher ground. The stovepipe stuck up through it, surrounded by dandelion leaves.

Ketty's garden, Tad thought wryly, as he ducked his head and walked in.

It was dark inside. The walls were smoothed and white-washed, and the earth floor was trodden firm, but the whole place smelt of damp, like an old cellar.

Ketty waited until they were all sitting down on the rough benches around the table. Then she looked across at Mr Jackson.

'You have papers that you would like to show me?'

'I think this will settle things.' Mr Jackson took out his wallet and carefully unfolded a battered document. 'It's perfectly straightforward.'

Ketty took it and spread it out on the table. Tad craned his head sideways to read over her shoulder.

I solemnly declare that I have this day received of Hannibal Henry Jackson the sum of five hundred dollars, in consideration of which I make over to him all my rights in the male Indian elephant known as Khush, together with my title to the said elephant's travelling vehicle and all equipment owned by me for the care and management of the said elephant.

> *(signed) Michael Keenan*
> *(witnessed) Esther Lanigan*

Cissie screwed her hands together. 'It's a forgery, isn't it, Ketty? Pa would never have sold Khush for five hundred dollars. And he never wrote in black ink.'

'I bought the ink specially,' Esther snapped. 'In Ginder Falls. And he was lucky to get five hundred dollars. With what we knew about him!'

Suddenly, there was complete silence in the dugout. Cissie stared at Esther, as though something new and unpleasant had come into her head. And Tad felt all sorts of things slipping into place.

'Mr Keenan told me it was blackmail,' he said slowly. 'And it was. You knew about the cripple trick, didn't you? *You saw him do it twice!*'

There was no need for them to answer. He could see from

181

their faces that he was right. Only Ketty looked bewildered for a second.

'The cripple trick?'

Tad pulled the little medicine bottle out of his pocket and put it in front of her. Immediately, she understood. She nodded sadly.

'He was lucky we were so kind.' Esther tossed her head. 'We could have got him arrested. And if they'd taken him back to Markle, he would have been lynched. But we actually gave him five hundred dollars.'

Ketty touched the little bottle with one finger. 'That was how Michael was,' she said softly. 'He liked to run risks. And then, when the danger came, he was not always . . . wise.'

Cissie almost exploded. 'But they blackmailed him. They broke the law!'

'*He* broke the law,' Mr Jackson said smoothly. 'Nothing else can be proved. Except that elephant is mine, and I've got Michael Keenan's signature to prove it.'

Ketty picked up the paper and took it to the door of the dugout, holding it sideways to the light. Her body blocked the entrance, and the rest of them sat in the shadows, waiting.

At last she came back to the table, sat down and pushed the paper back towards Mr Jackson. 'I know Mr Keenan's writing very well. And I think that he wrote this.'

'Ketty! How can you say—?'

Cissie jumped up, but Ketty put a hand on her shoulder and pulled her down again.

'I *must* say it, Cissie—because it is true. How many times must I tell you it is no good to lie to yourself? If you look at the paper with honest eyes, you will know that your father wrote his name there.'

Mr Jackson took back the receipt and Esther stood up.

'That's all sorted out, then. We'll take what's ours and say no more about the trouble we've been put to.'

Ketty looked at her, with steady eyes. 'You would do better to sit down, Miss Lanigan, and listen to me.'

'There's nothing more to say.' Esther scowled. 'You agreed with us! You said that was Michael Keenan's signature.'

182

Cissie muttered under her breath, and Ketty smiled suddenly, the very faintest of smiles. 'I believe that that is Michael Keenan's signature. And that the receipt makes over to Mr Jackson all Michael Keenan's rights to Khush.'

'Well, then—'

'I think—' Ketty's gaze shifted to Mr Jackson. 'I think that you do not remember Michael Keenan as well as I remember his signature. He was not—a straightforward man.'

Suddenly, Mr Jackson was very, very still. 'What do you mean?'

'I mean that you paid him a great deal more than his rights to Khush were worth.'

'Explain yourself.' He was motionless, his eyes fixed on Ketty's face. Esther sank back on to the bench.

Ketty slid open the drawer of the table and pulled out a tin box. Then she smiled up at them. 'You are not the only one who has papers, Mr Jackson. I, too. I think that you should see mine.'

She opened the lid of the box and sorted through the papers inside until she found the ones she wanted. Not scrawled notes, like Mr Jackson's receipt, but proper legal documents, drawn up in a lawyer's handwriting. As she unfolded the crackling paper, Tad's eyes skimmed over the words.

The first was a transfer of ownership of the male Indian elephant known as Khush, from Puddifoot's Circus to Miss Kerstin Gilstring.

The second was an agreement between Mrs Kerstin Svensson (née Gilstring) and Mr Michael Keenan. It gave Michael Keenan the right to any money raised by the performances of the elephant known as Khush, in return for which he was to maintain the elephant in good condition. But he was specifically prohibited from selling or exchanging the elephant in any way, or from giving it in settlement of a gambling debt.

'Michael Keenan was my business partner,' Ketty said. 'I knew him very well.'

She pushed the papers over the table to Mr Jackson, but he didn't bother to read them. He went on staring at her.

'What are these papers? What do they mean?'

Ketty folded her hands. 'They mean, Mr Jackson, that you couldn't have bought Khush from Michael Keenan. Because Michael Keenan never owned him. He belongs to me.'

Esther drew in her breath, sharply. The air was electric. Tad watched Mr Jackson's face and waited for an explosion.

But it was Cissie who jumped to her feet. Cissie who shrieked, at the top of her voice:

'But that's dreadful! I can't bear it! It's ruined everything!'

Blindly, stumbling into the earth wall and the edge of the door, she charged away from the table and out of the dugout.

CHAPTER 30

'DON'T GO! It's all right!'

Everyone else was speechless, but Tad jumped up from the table and raced after Cissie.

She was walking down the slope towards the creek.

'It's all right,' he called again, slithering after her. 'It won't make any difference.'

Cissie glared over her shoulder. 'What are you talking about?' She sounded fierce, but he could see that she was crying.

'It doesn't matter,' Tad said. 'That Khush doesn't belong to you. He's—he's—'

He looked sideways. Khush had lifted his head and he was watching them both with his small, calm eyes. There was no way of describing everything that he was.

'He doesn't have to belong to you,' Tad said, harshly. 'He'll be here, where you are. That's the important thing.'

Cissie sniffed and rubbed her sleeve across her face. 'That's not it at all. I don't want Khush to be here.'

'But I thought—' Tad grabbed her shoulders and pulled her round to face him. 'I thought that was what we were doing. Bringing Khush here. I've grovelled in a coal barge, and crouched on a boiler deck, and swum in the Missouri—*to help you to keep Khush.* I thought you wanted him. The way I—'

He bit the words off short and walked away. Khush looked up from the pool where he was standing and Tad went into the water, ankle-deep, and laid his head against that soft, solid flank. Lifting his trunk, Khush blew, very gently, on to Tad's cheek.

Cissie stared down into the creek. 'I didn't want Khush. I needed him. I was going to sell him and give Ketty the money, so that I could stay here.'

'*Sell* him?'

'Of course. But I can't, because—' Cissie's voice cracked. '—because he's hers already. I haven't got anything to give her.' She sat down on the bank and leaned her head on her knees.

Tad frowned. 'Why do you need anything to give her? She won't want to be paid. I thought—'

'What did you think?' Cissie muttered.

He'd thought he understood about Ketty. *She was like a mother to me*, Cissie had said. And that first hug, out on the prairie, had been as tender as any mother's. How could Cissie talk about money? About paying?

What was she paying for?

The question came from the back of Tad's brain, so sharply it knocked the breath out of him.

'It doesn't work,' he said softly. 'However much you pay. It's never enough.'

Cissie blinked up at him. 'Enough for what?'

'Enough for whatever you've done.' Tad closed his eyes, discovering what he had always known without knowing it. 'My aunt took me in, when I was a baby. Looked after me like a mother, everyone said. I worked and worked for her, but it was never enough to make up for—for what I'd done.'

He heard Cissie breathe in, sharply. 'What did you do?'

'My mother should never have had a baby.' Tad swallowed. 'She died when I was born. Because of me. And whatever I did was never enough to pay for killing Linnie Hawkins.'

'*That* wasn't your fault!' Cissie said. 'Your aunt can't have loved you much. Not if she let you think that.'

The words rattled in Tad's brain like the last pieces of a jigsaw. He couldn't fit them into his own puzzle, but he offered them back to Cissie.

'And if Ketty loves you—'

'You don't understand.' Cissie's eyes slid away from his. 'I—'

For a moment, Tad thought she was going to stop there. Then she took a quick, short breath and spoke very fast.

'I made Olivia give me the seat by the window. It was her turn, but I nagged and nagged. And when the crash came, I went through the window, and—' She screwed up her fists and looked fiercely at Tad. 'I didn't mean to! It wasn't my *fault!*'

It was no use saying that. Tad had tried it himself, over and over again. Lying awake in bed, staring at the dark ceiling. *It wasn't my fault, it wasn't my fault.* It never worked.

But suddenly he knew what would. 'You must tell Ketty. *She* won't let you think it's your fault.'

Cissie shivered. 'But I haven't got anything to give her.'

'That doesn't matter. You must trust her.'

'But—' Cissie twisted her hands together and stared down at the knuckles. Then she spoke in a stiff, tight voice, forcing out the words as though she were choking. 'What about you, Tad? Do *you* think it was my fault? Do *you* think I killed Olivia?'

'What does it matter what *I* think?' Tad said.

Cissie didn't answer. She just went on staring down at her knuckles. But she held her back very straight and her cheeks were scarlet.

What does it matter what I think? Inside Tad's head, the certainties shifted, like great blocks of stone. The air between them seemed to crackle, and he was afraid to speak.

But he dared not stay silent. 'You didn't kill anyone,' he said slowly. 'It was an accident. Just like my mother's death.'

Cissie went on staring down. 'Is that what you really think?'

'Yes, of course it is.' Suddenly it was easy. Tad waded down the creek until he was standing in front of her. Catching her chin, he pulled her round to look at him. 'Everything's all right, Cissie. You're alive, and you didn't kill Olivia, and you're here at Ketty's.'

He felt her relax, very slightly, as she met his eyes. 'And Ketty will let me stay here?'

Tad grinned. 'Just you try running off!'

Slowly, a smile began to spread over Cissie's face.

But before she could say anything, there was a loud, angry noise in the doorway of the dugout. Mr Jackson strode through, pulling Hjalmar after him. He was in a towering, terrifying rage. His massive fingers gripped Hjalmar's wrist, tugging him down the slope towards the creek.

Esther came next, picking her way fastidiously through the dust, and then Ketty, holding the little medicine bottle in one hand.

'Now!' Mr Jackson said. His voice was like sharpened steel. 'We'll make sure your husband understands what you're turning down, Mrs Svensson. Even if he doesn't understand English, he can understand what he sees. And anyone can tell that he could use five hundred dollars.'

He pulled the money out of his pocket and turned to Hjalmar, letting him see how much it was. Then he held it out to Ketty.

'I've paid once, but I'm prepared to pay again. This is for you, Mrs Svensson.'

He pointed at the money, and then at Ketty, glancing at Hjalmar, to make sure that he understood.

'I want to buy the elephant.'

He pointed first at Khush and then at himself. Then he flapped the hand that held the money. And waited.

Ketty looked at the money. Slowly and deliberately, she put her hands behind her back. 'My elephant is not for sale, Mr Jackson.'

No one could have mistaken the meaning. Mr Jackson looked triumphantly at Hjalmar.

'You see what she's doing? Are you going to let her get away with it? The elephant's no use to you, but your farm needs this.'

He stood square and solid, holding out his money. Confident that Hjalmar would side with him, now he knew what was going on.

Hjalmar looked quickly from the money to the elephant and then across to Mr Jackson. He glanced at Ketty and raised one eyebrow, checking that he had understood right.

Then he stepped forward and knocked Mr Jackson down, with one hard, straight blow to the chin.

'*Du får lov att gå nu,*' he said, very politely.

Esther shrieked and stepped backwards, and Mr Jackson growled at them from where he lay, sprawled in the water.

'What's that supposed to mean?'

Ketty looked down, with the very faintest of smiles. 'I think my husband wants you to go away, and stop bothering me.'

Mr Jackson levered his huge body out of the water and took a step towards her. 'If you can't see what a chance you're missing—'

But he got no further. Because Khush lifted his trunk and squirted him, full in the face.

And he didn't stop there. He dipped his trunk into the creek and lifted it up again to squirt Esther, catching her bonnet, so that water dripped and trickled down from her feathers. She screamed and picked up her skirts.

'I'm not staying in this horrible place!'

Mr Jackson seized her arm. 'Wait. I'm not in the habit of giving up—'

The next squirt caught him in the stomach, drenching his clothes. Ketty smiled gravely.

'I think you will *have* to give up, Mr Jackson. Even if I agreed to sell Khush, it would be no use. *He refuses to belong to you.*'

As if he understood, Khush came lumbering out of the water towards Esther. With a terrible, ear-splitting yell, she picked up her skirts and ran for her horse, screaming at Mr Jackson to follow.

But he had something else to say. Pulling himself up to his full height, ignoring the water that dripped from every part of him, he glared at Ketty.

'Whatever you say now, ma'am, you'll be forced to sell that elephant to someone. Maybe these—these *children*—don't understand how unsuitable the plains are for an elephant, but you know very well. My offer's withdrawn, and I think you will regret turning me down.'

Ketty raised her eyebrows. 'I do not think so. Khush is mine, and I shall decide what is best to do with him. But this, I think, is yours.' She stretched out her hand, offering him the medicine bottle. 'You bought whatever Michael Keenan owned for the care of the elephant. And this is all that remains.'

Mr Jackson snorted impatiently and knocked the bottle

into a clump of grass. 'I'm not staying while you make fun of me—'

He stamped off after Esther and the two of them mounted their horses and rode away. No one spoke until they had dwindled into tiny figures, moving towards the horizon.

Then Cissie looked down at the little bottle. It lay tilted, catching the last rays of the sun, so that the liquid inside swirled like clouded jade. 'Ketty—'

Ketty was watching her. 'It is time to talk,' she said quietly. 'And Hjalmar too, maybe. If Tad will excuse us.'

Tad nodded, and the three of them walked away from him, up the slope. As they reached the doorway, Cissie glanced back at Tad. For a second, he saw her face, pale against the darkness of the dugout. Then Ketty slipped an arm round her shoulders and led her inside.

Suddenly, the whole prairie was quite silent. No one spoke. Nothing moved. Tad was nothing but a small speck in the middle of the great flat emptiness. He stared up at the closed door of the dugout and the clumped green leaves of the dandelions on the roof above.

Then Khush flapped his ears, expectantly, and Tad rounded on him.

'It's no use looking at me! I can't stay here with you. And I can't take you away with me—'

They seemed the bleakest words in the world and, now that they were spoken, there was no point in saying anything else. Tad walked along the bank to where he had heaped their bundles and found the old, stiff brush he used for scrubbing. Then he untied Khush's tethers and led him out of the water.

'Move up. Move up, there.'

Khush lumbered on to the bank and stood very still, knowing what was coming. Tad found the bucket and dipped some water from the creek.

Then he started to scrub.

He began, very carefully, with Khush's head, running the brush over the top of the broad, strong skull and down on to the massive sweep of his back, with its sprinkling of sandy hair.

Then he worked on the soft, wrinkled skin at the side,

running his hands over it to feel that it was clean. Then round the tail and the rump, and down the long, solid legs.

He scrubbed every inch, and as he scrubbed he stored up the feel and the smell of it, and the sound the brush made as it travelled over and round and down. Because this would be the last time.

Tonight he would sleep down by the creek, with Khush. And in the morning he would go away, very quickly, while he could still bear the thought of walking, on his own, across the empty prairie.

He scrubbed until there was no more to scrub. Then he dropped the brush and let his head fall forwards, leaning against Khush's trunk as it curled round to support him.

It was almost dark when Ketty came to find him. She walked down from the dugout on her own and stopped a few feet away, leaving Tad the privacy of the shadows.

'You are very good,' she said quietly. 'To bring Cissie safe here.'

'A pleasure,' Tad muttered. 'She brought herself, mostly.'

Ketty chuckled. Then she bent down and picked up something from the grass. 'It is wonderful, is it not? Cissie and this little bottle—they are both fragile, and both have travelled so far, unbroken.'

She came down the slope towards Tad, and Khush rumbled softly, stretching his trunk out towards her.

'I am happy to see you again, dear Khush.' She laid a hand on his side. 'But you cannot stay here. This is no place for an elephant.' Tad caught his breath and she glanced sideways at him. 'You understand that, I think?'

'I—yes, ma'am.' He could hardly trust himself to speak.

Ketty turned the bottle in her hands, looking down thoughtfully. 'Khush must travel. I should sell him to someone who will take him from place to place, to find good weather, and to amaze new people. This land is so wide that he can travel for all his life and never be done.'

Wide. Tad's head whirled. They had come two thousand

miles, but still there was almost a whole country left untravelled. From the goldfields of California to the everglades of Florida. From the elegance of New Orleans to the Indian tepees of Dakota. In his mind, he saw Khush striding across a huge map, his feet stepping delicately from state to state.

And he thought, *I won't even know where he is.*

He wished Ketty would finish and go away. But she didn't. She came much closer. So close that he could smell the faint, clean scent of her clothes in the still air. Gently, she put a hand on his shoulder.

'Who shall I find to buy him?'

'I guess—' Tad's voice croaked in his throat and the words came out roughly. 'Someone with a lot of money, ma'am.'

Through the shadows, he saw her smile. 'Khush can make his own money. Maybe I could trust someone to take him and send me money every month. Do you think that would be a good plan?'

'I—'

Tad swallowed. Ketty stood waiting, tilting the medicine bottle backwards and forwards in her hands. It was too dark to see anything distinctly. For a second, in the shadows, Tad almost heard the swish of great trees overhead. Almost caught the heavy scent of overblown white roses and the gleam of the white frame house, masked by the green shade of the imagined garden.

Ketty chuckled again. 'Do you think I have a choice? That I can sell my elephant to anyone I choose?'

'Ma'am?'

'I think you should leave now. Without Khush.'

Tad stared at her, mystified, and she laughed softly. Then she pulled the cork from the bottle in her hands. He heard the faint pop as it came out. And then a long, slow trickle as all the liquid ran out on to the ground.

'The end of the medicine show,' she said, and her voice was quiet and sad. 'No more tricks. It is time to find out the truth.' She gave Tad a little push. 'Off you go. Away across the prairie.'

As if he were dreaming, Tad began to walk. Across the

creek and up into the unknown country beyond, walking west in the darkness. Taking one step after another that separated him from Khush.

Over his head, the enormous prairie sky spread in a great dome, full of remote stars, and he walked on and on, into the vast space and the terror of emptiness. He was more frightened than he had ever been. If things went wrong now, he could never turn back. He would go on walking across the plains until he dropped.

But he went no more than two hundred yards. Then there was a thunder of feet behind him, and a loud elephant roar. Khush came charging up from the creek, with his trunk outstretched and his mouth wide open, furious at being left behind.

Before he had stopped moving, he caught Tad up and swung him high into the air. For an instant, Tad was suspended in darkness, with nothing to keep him from falling except Khush's strong grey trunk.

He had never felt so safe in all his life.

Then Khush swung him round, and Tad scrambled on to his back, feeling for places to grip with his knees and hands.

Ketty's voice came from across the creek. 'You see, Tad? You see what has to be?'

And from higher up the slope, there was a loud, jubilant shout. Tad looked over his shoulder and saw a small, determined figure standing on the roof of the dugout, waving both arms in triumph.

'Everything's all right, Tad! We've got here! You've got Khush! And everything's going to be *wonderful*!'

Tad wanted to shout back, but he couldn't speak, because a great yell of joy was gathering in his throat. He opened his mouth and let it come, bellowing a single word out across the prairie.

'KHUSH!'

In front of him, the great grey ears flapped and over his shoulder, from behind, came a warm, fresh wind. Blowing towards the west.